In the twilight haze, a lone flyer came sharply into ew. Sitting on the fire escape, Benjamin had been eping watch for just this event all afternoon. Every loose ip of paint had been picked off the metal railing by en's nervous fingers. Without ceremony, he removed the tter and drank in the paper's words:

Benjamin:

It sounds like you and the "kids" had a good party. Believe e, I was there in spirit. May you have many, many, more. As to my handwriting - keep your Cross pen, thank you very uch. My fountain pen is much more expressive of me. Your modern folks" line sent me giggling; and this comes from a man ho still uses a 25 year old black and white TV. When are u going to join the modern world of color? Enough said! I ame the new nib of my pen on the blotches; it still needs to be ken in more. In truth, I have been a bit ill this week, but not worry, I'm seeing the doctor today. I should be back to my- f in no time.

With care and prayers,
Maddie

The letter did not seem to contain any menacing formation. Why then did Benjamin feel such a fleeting, t unmistakable, dread race through his heart?

Padwolf Publishing books by
Hunter Lord & Ariel Masters

EVERMORE
WOMBERS AND INNUENDOES

EVERMORE

Hunter Lord

Hunter Lord & Ariel Masters

PADWOLF PUBLISHING

VISIT OUR WEBSITE AT:
HTTP://iypn.com/padwolfpub

EVERMORE

Publisher: PADWOLF PUBLISHING
Authors: Hunter Lord & Ariel Masters

Cover Artist: Jeff Smith
Editor-In-Chief: Diane Raetz
Creative Director: William E. Ecay
Book Editor: Marie Perry
Promotions/PR Director: Richard Bukowski

PADWOLF PUBLISHING™
457 Main Street, Suite 384
Farmingdale, NY 11735

ISBN: 1-890096-01-6

Printed in the United States of America

10 9 8 7 6 5 4 3 2 1

For The Wench
-HL

For the future, and to the hope that lives in all who love...
-AM

CARRIER PIGEON

Maddie,

Haven't heard from you in weeks. Getting worried. You were due back from your daughter's on Monday. Babe has brought back three messages untouched since then. Please reply ASAP so that I know all is well.

Benjamin

Maddie gently smiled as she scanned the note. Her ability to read between the lines was not needed with this letter, Benjamin was clearly frantic. She had only been gone for three extra days, due to her daughter's catching the flu. Ben's concern touched and warmed her heart.

Ben rarely admitted his true feelings, even to her. Although she had saved all their correspondence, the few notes in which he wrote of his feelings toward her, were placed prominently in her collection. She treasured their contents over the years.

They were the only two of their original group left; four of the old gang had passed on in the last couple of years alone. The sad thing was that few of the younger generation seemed interested in learning about their life-long passion for raising and training homing pigeons. The young just did not appreciate either the beauty of the birds or the intimacy of the written word - why bother, when phones were so easy to use. A fax machine was infinitely quicker than tying a note to a pigeon's leg and having it soar skyward. What a loss the young's efficiency had cost them, Maddie mourned.

Benjamin hated any modern machinery and refused to have even a phone, much less a fax machine, in his loft. He grudgingly accepted the fact that Maddie owned a phone, but she still kept secret her fax. She sent letters regularly to her daughters and grandkids via the machine. Her birds just did not have the speed or endurance to make a run from Boston to Miami. The fax was just about the only secret she kept from her friend.

Stepping onto her balcony, she greeted her brood; five rotund, cooing, soarers. Caring for her birds never failed to awaken something almost spiritual in her. After proper salutations to each one, Maddie gently pulled out her favorite, Angel.

In his coal-black eyes shone a spark of recognition and he settled quietly in her hands. She folded the letter and placed it on the bird's leg. Holding him aloft, she whispered, "Fly to him, sweet messenger." Obediently, Angel rose heavenward. She stood a moment watching, then turned and went inside.

Angel's flight carried him south over the city of Boston to a large third-story loft in Hyde Park. Benjamin was anxiously awaiting the message's arrival. His impatience in waiting for a reply was making him antsy: the pigeon cages were being cleaned for the fourth time that week. He was running low on newspapers and might actually be forced to buy some, instead of waiting for his neighbors to throw theirs out.

Finally, Angel landed with a flourish at the open window and strutted to the cages that Ben had built into the corner of the loft. With great tenderness, he removed, unwrapped, and read the note.

Benjamin:

My deepest apologies; my delay was unavoidable, I assure you. Leslie came down with a terrible case of the flu, and with little Jeanie's confirmation that Sunday, there was too much work for the poor dear to do alone. So I stayed and baby-sat until she was over it. In defense, I told Tony to send you a short note if I was delayed. I'm afraid my youthful neighbor is not good with directions, but at least my babies don't starve when I'm gone. I'm tired, but glad to be home.

Awaiting Your Reply,
Maddie

Nodding as he reread the note several times, Benjamin finally ended his study with a grunt of satisfaction. He stroked Angel's back. Shutting the coop's door, he moved to the living section of the loft, note in hand.

Although not clearly defined as "living room", "dining room", etc., there was a logic in the arrangement of his living quarters. There was a boundary of cleanliness surrounding the coop, for sanitation's sake; the rest of the loft had the freeform air of a typical life-long bachelor's apartment: most of the clothes in the sleeping/dressing area, most of the food and eating utensils in the kitchen/living area. Even with the surface messiness, there was a Spartan atmosphere to the place.

Benjamin settled on his couch with paper and pen and after a brief glance at Maddie's words, began his reply.

The following morning, Maddie was interrupted during her morning cup of coffee by a familiar fluttering of wings. Peeking out her French doors, she was greeted by the cocky strutting of Dizzy Dean along her balcony's railings. He boldly proceeded to the coop, where he settled in amongst his friends and brethren.

Quickly finishing her coffee, Maddie dabbed her mouth and stepped outside. Picking up Dizzy Dean, her nose was tickled by an unfamiliar odor. "What have you been in, D.D?" she thought. As she read the letter, she unsuccessfully stifled a giggle.

Maddie;

Apology accepted. Don't worry a minute about it; glad to hear all is well. Give Leslie my best and congratulations to Jeanie. John and his ilk were by yesterday. Ever since his father died, they have been treating me as more of a father/grandfather than uncle. Gave me a necktie - useless, I never wear them - and aftershave for my birthday. Of course, I already have twelve bottles of the stuff. Can't even smell it over the birds and Lysol. I put a dab behind Dizzy dean's neck for you to smell. What do you think?

                            Benjamin

"You silly old thing," Maddie mused. "This is the first time that you've done anything like this. Of course, I've periodically scented my letters for some time; he's never commented on it but apparently his sense of smell isn't too deadened to not have noticed. Poor babies! Dizzy Dean's got you sneezing." Gabriel and Babe were huddled in the corner, puffed up and miserable-looking, and the others were blinking and a-chooing in tiny, fitful bursts.

"Well, D.D., you stink, so I'm afraid you're making the return run today. One minute, love." She sat at her kitchen table and quickly penned a reply. Maddie paused briefly as she folded it, considering whether to add cologne this time. Deciding that it would be gilding the lily, she passed on adding any further insult to D.D.'s nose.

Upon standing, Maddie felt somewhat dizzy and clutched at her chair. "Slow down, gal; you'll be feeling your age if you don't. I must be catching Leslie's bug." Within a minute or so, Maddie was feeling better. Slowly walking to the balcony, she placed the letter on Dizzy Dean, released him, then went inside to lie down a bit.

Scanning the heavens like a farmer looking for rain, Benjamin stood in front of the window. Humming tunelessly, he ran the dishwater and cleaned up his single place setting. "The advantage of living alone is that you don't have much to clean up," he wryly thought to himself. Not that having additional housecleaning would be a worthwhile tradeoff at times, but I guess that a lifetime of habits would tax the patience of the best of women...the best...

Suddenly snapped out of his daydreaming, Benjamin's eyes caught the incoming silhouette of a pigeon. As soon as Dizzy Dean landed, the bird was relieved of his cargo.

Dear Benjamin:

A "dab" indeed! I thank you for the sample to sniff, but the birds appeared to dislike it. A star on your chart for the thought though. Not to sound like I'm nagging, but you know that John and his family truly care for you. And we both know that you feel the same toward them, if you weren't too stubborn to admit it. I'm going to keep this short, as I'm going to indulge in one of the few luxuries of old age and take an afternoon nap.

Fondly,
Maddie

P.S. Thanks for the subtle hint, but I haven't forgotten your birthday. I'll send Babe back with your gift Saturday.

Maddie's nap became an all night affair with her pillow. She did not awake until 7:30 AM, almost an hour past her usual rising with the dawn. By the end of breakfast, she was humming old show tunes, entertaining her heavenly messengers, and generally back to her old self. After straightening an already immaculate living room, she opened a well oiled drawer of an ancient dresser. Removing the contents of a stationary box, she sat down at her writing desk with fountain pen and paper.

An hour or so later, Maddie was ready to send off her special Air Delivery. Like the Pony Express of old, Babe was "saddled up" and sent off. He made the trek in record time, despite the extra baggage. Babe's arrival coincided with the start of Benjamin's birthday feast: filet mignon, medium rare, baked potato with sour cream, corn on the cob, and home style biscuits - or so the package claimed. Each pigeon took part in the feast, indulging in some high grade bird seed. Benjamin opened Maddie's note and read as he ate in between smiles.

HAPPY BIRTHDAY!

Well, well, you made it: three-quarters of a century! Now quit groaning, youngster; I have no sympathy with people grumbling about their age. I personally cherish every moment added to my life. Every additional year builds upon my growing library of bittersweet experiences - I'm happy to count you among those times.

Enclosed is a gift certificate for the book store two blocks down from you. The amount is for that book on Baseball Greats that you had mentioned in the past. I know that you'll enjoy the chapters on the Yankees and the Red Sox. Also expect a cake delivery sometime this evening. Dark chocolate with slivers of burnt almonds - your favorite, I believe. Enjoy! I'd better stop now or Babe will get a hernia from delivering this.

Affectionately yours,
Maddie

Benjamin felt very full, not only with his birthday meal, but also with the attention of his friend. Loosening his belt and leaning back in his chair, he thought to himself, its moments like this that make living this long worthwhile.

"Thank goodness for Tony! I don't know what I would have done without him these past few days; he's been keeping you all healthy," Maddie apologized to her pigeons, uncharacteristically still in her gown at 10:00 AM. Her kitchen table was covered in various over the counter potions, used in an attempt to ease the numerous symptoms which had attacked her of late. The first two days she put it down as the flu: chills and fever, nausea, the usual. But other problems began: trembling periods, blurring vision, sores on her arms and abdomen, times when her tongue would cleave to her mouth and her lips would crack.

She picked up her calendar, noting that her doctor's appointment was at 2:00 today. Lord, she hated doctors with a passion and had managed to avoid them for most of her life, but not today. She had also managed to avoid most of Benjamin's questioning this past week, but he was persistent. She reread the letter that he sent regarding his birthday:

Maddie:

Thanks for your kind gift. Babe had no problem bringing it; good thing you did not send the book itself. Ha, Ha! I went and got the book this morning; it is marvelous. Has trivia even I did not know. The cake was delicious. We all enjoyed it; I gave each of the feathered "kids" a small piece. I wish you could have had some. Got to go. Time to begin working on my next quarter century. Take care and thanks again.

                    Benjamin

P.S. Noticed that your usually superb penmanship was a bit shaky today. Your fountain pen actually left blotches. Why not join the rest of us modern folk and use a ball-point? I have an extra Cross pen I can give you; I got it one year instead of a tie.

"Bless him," she gently smiled. "He constantly surprises me - noticing my handwriting. I can't have him worrying about me." Gathering her writing supplies, she began.

In the twilight haze, a lone flyer came sharply into view. Sitting on the fire escape, Benjamin had been keeping watch for just this event all afternoon. Every loose chip of paint had been picked off the metal railing by Ben's nervous fingers. Without ceremony, he removed the letter and drank in the paper's words:

Benjamin:

It sounds like you and the "kids" had a good party. Believe me, I was there in spirit. May you have many, many, more. As to my handwriting - keep your Cross pen, thank you very much. My fountain pen is much more expressive of me. Your "modern folks" line sent me giggling; this comes from a man who still uses a 25 year old black and white TV. When are you going to join the modern world of color? Enough said! I blame the new nib of my pen on the blotches; it still needs to be broken in more. In truth, I have been a bit ill this week, but not to worry, I'm seeing the doctor today. I should be back to myself in no time.

With care and prayers,
Maddie

The letter did not seem to contain any menacing information. Why then did Benjamin feel such a fleeting, yet unmistakable, dread race through his heart?

Maddie may have been the one visiting the doctor, but you would have thought it was him by Benjamin's behavior. His pacing would have driven Maddie crazy had she witnessed it. When she returned home that evening, Dizzy Dean was waiting on the balcony with a short and direct question:

Maddie:
How did it go?

Benjamin

Maddie stared at the note in her hands. The last thing she wanted to do was to worry Ben, but she needed to talk to someone. Her usual optimism did not talk her out of the feeling that something was terribly, terribly wrong.

Benjamin:

It's not the flu. The doctor said that he wasn't sure what it was. He had read about something similar in a journal of medicine, but did not want to say anything until he had more information. They ran a lot of tests, including taking a ton of blood. I must go back in 3 days.

Deepest Affection,
Maddie

After the initial doctor's visit, the usual frequent correspondence between the two did not seem often enough. Maddie was not the kind of woman who worried needlessly, and her own concern for herself caused Benjamin to attempt to quiet her fears, and his own.

Maddie:

Sorry to hear that in this day and age the medical establishment can remain ignorant. With luck, he just had a slow week and needed your extra tests to perk up his sagging income. So don't worry; you are as strong as a mule. When you are feeling better, you can prove it to yourself by pulling me in my grandnephew's wagon from Quincy Market to the Commons like one of those horse drawn carriage rides. If you do that I may even give you a carrot. Ha, Ha!

All my best,
Benjamin

Benjamin:

Mule indeed, you're more like one, you stubborn old coot. As for a carrot...I'd settle for nothing less than strawberry cheesecake after a job like that. But thanks for the smile. I went to the doctor again today. He thought I might have that awful HIV or even the start of AIDS, but the blood test was negative, so he took even more blood for even more tests. Damn vampire! He says it's something to do with my total immune system shutting down. I'm scared, Benjamin. Say a prayer for me please.

Unconditionally,
Maddie

Dear Maddie:

The priest down at St. Joseph's nearly called the fire department on me. I lit up an entire rack of candles for you. Yes, I know I'm Lutheran, but you're Catholic, so I figured God might listen better in your church. I talked and pleaded with him all last night; I hope he listens. After all, you're the keeper of His angels. Please be well.

Affectionately,
Benjamin

Benjamin:

I finally have a name for what I have.

They are calling it *TADS*, which stands for *Transmitted Adenosine deaminase Deficiency Syndrome*. Anyway, you remember that old movie about the "Boy in the Bubble"? Apparently it is like an adult equivalent caused by a virus. They don't know how I got it or where it came from. There has been two or three dozen cases of it in the past several months in Boston alone.

My dear Ben, for the rest of my news you had better be sitting down. From what they tell me I'm certain to not be able to survive in the "real" world. I will have to go to a sterile treatment center. There are only three in the country: in New York, L.A., and New Orleans.

I would be shutoff from all that I love. I couldn't bring my babies of course. I would never be allowed out to hold my daughters or grandkids again. I told them to stuff it. I've had a full life. If it is my time to go, I want to go here at home...I'm too old to adjust.

They give me three to nine months, maybe less because of my age. Remember when eighty three used to be young? Time for my nap; I hate to have to take it, but it's needed now.

With extreme fondness,
Maddie

Maddie:

Pardon me for speaking like this to a truly great lady, but ARE YOU NUTS? Damn it, you should live as long as you can, no matter what. Move to New York; true, its not as nice as Boston, but a city that could produce the Yankees of old must have a lot going for it. I know it sounds terrible, but it could be okay.

I'll take care of your angels (except for any you want Tony to have). Don't think me mad, but we could still keep up our correspondence. I know they won't let the pigeons in but they would let you have a fax. I hate the damn things but for you I would hardly notice the sacrifice. Please reconsider.

Your loyal friend,
Benjamin

Benjamin:

I appreciate the sentiment, but no matter what, I'm staying put. I won't die in a strange place. Please understand and respect my wishes. I, of all people, know that it is hard, but this is how it has to be.

Your extremely dear friend,
Maddie

After several of these rounds of emotional bombings, Benjamin was reeling from the shock waves. In a very short time, his friend and constant joy appeared to be disappearing from his world. He was beginning to be acutely aware of how much a part of his life Maddie was, and of how dark that same existence would become without her.

He started hounding the medical library at Harvard, begging for any information on this terrible TADS which had captured and was feverishly devouring Maddie day by day. He plowed through polysyllablic medical journals, written soundbites produced to calm the troubled masses, and hysterical tabloid rantings.

He learned of the label "Innuendo" given to the cloistered survivors in the bubbles, courtesy of the American press: a small child commenting on people she had seen in the bubble said that they were living "in 'da windows" - "Inn-u-endo". Benjamin snorted at the feeble attempt at cuteness given to a dying people. Few people wanted to stare into the ugly face of this tragedy; if the press could sanitize the problem, they would. On the other hand, Benjamin tried to beat the monster back with all the knowledge he could find.

What he found gave him little hope: article after article spoke of the steady march toward death the victims walked. He became intimately familiar with the many signs and symptoms: how each person differed in the way the disease seemed to effect the immune system - some died quickly, others lingered for months. The only common thread tying all together was that the lungs were the area always attacked first.

So the disease was probably airborne; so why had he not caught it? True, he and Maddie lived on opposite sides of town, but the air quality couldn't be that different, could it? In any case, the cause was a moot point for him - he was not looking for causes, but solutions! But the magic potion apparently did not yet exist.

Benjamin's life was divided into three parts: if he was not caring for his birds, or writing to Maddie, he spent hours rereading every scrap of correspondence she had ever sent him. As he thought and fumed with impotence at his inability to assist her in her time of need, his heart began admitting to his head what was always known, but never fully acknowledged - he loved her. At this late stage in his life, without having ever met or touched one another, she was more a part of him than many life-long marriages. He must convey this to her. The sheer power of this revelation had to keep death at bay!

On the way home from the library that evening, his eye was caught by a flash of light from a peddler's cart. Peering more closely, he saw that the cart displayed a multitude of carved crystal necklaces and paperweights. The face of one of the necklaces caused him to gasp aloud, "That's it! "

Gently swaying among the other baubles was a dainty crystal heart with a soaring bird carved on it. Almost trembling, Benjamin pulled it off the rack and examined it.

"That dove symbolizes the Holy Spirit inside the Christian heart," the peddler droned, obviously reciting the pat description. Benjamin stared at the tiny item in his hand, thinking, "Yes, that... but to Maddie and I it would be even more... with this, I can literally give my heart to her. Its perfect; I'll take it." He quickly paid the man without even blinking at the price and rushed home, cradling it close to his chest.

No sooner had Benjamin closed his apartment door behind him, the door to the coop flew open at his touch. Babe was unceremoniously escorted out. A note, hastily written on the bus home, was attached to one leg; the crystal heart was anchored to the other. Lopsided, Babe took to the air, on a mission of romance.

Babe landed on the balcony, waking Maddie from her late afternoon slumber. Tony was there, trying to silently deliver her mail without disturbing her rest. Slowly opening her eyes, Maddie first caught sight of Tony and weakly smiled her hello. Her eyes then grew wider as she saw Babe. With great effort, she rolled sideways on the couch and pushed herself into a sitting position.

Seeing the strain in her face, Tony motioned her to stay seated. "I'll get him, Maddie; you rest."

"Pish-posh! I may be sick, but I can still walk. Besides," she feebly quipped, "This should be getting easier, since I'm ten pounds lighter this week." Refusing to cater to her failing limbs, she arose. Holding a finely carved cane her son-in-law had recently given her, she shakily covered the short distance to Babe.

"Babe, what did your father do to you, you poor thing." Removing both bundles from the pigeon, she turned to sit in a chair on her balcony. As she passed by the glass doors, a spasm of coughing racked her body, almost knocking her to the floor. Tony moved to help her, but Maddie waved him away. Looking down at the handkerchief she had covered her mouth with, she grimaced at the mixture of mucus and blood. No matter how many times it happened, it still surprised her.

"Maddie, perhaps it would be better if you stayed inside. There are a lot more germs out there. The light's better for reading in here, anyway."

"Nonsense! I want to read Benjamin's note here and have the setting sun's last warmth bathe my face. When I'm in that pine box, it's going to be dark enough - no twilight there." Maddie spoke in her determined way and that was that. Tony knew better than to attempt an argument he could not win, so he wished her goodnight and left her mail on the coffee table.

Maddie sat with Benjamin's offerings in her lap. Remembering the manners her mother had taught her, she read the letter before opening her gift.

Maddie:

I've been doing a lot of thinking lately. (You know how hard that is for me and my failing memory: they say the memory is the second thing to go - wish I could remember the first. Sorry, old joke from an old fool.)

One thing I could never forget is you, my dear lady, or the times and shared memories we have. I want you to have this gift as a token of my affection.

She slipped the crumpled wrapping off the necklace. The heart's facets caught the cascading rays of the setting sun. The shining light mirrored the gleam of tears forming in Maddie's eyes.

The letter continued:

Once I saw it I thought of you, Maddie. The fool selling it tried to tell me that it was a dove, but I can clearly see that it is a pigeon - looks a lot like your Angel, don't you think? I want to tell you the conclusion I've reached, but for once I don't want to write... I want to tell you, face to face.

Will be at your door tomorrow morning, at nine o'clock. See you then.

With love,
Benjamin

"Sweet Benjamin, you romantic, you. After all this time, its finally happening. Such bitter irony it took this...but thank you Lord, for this moment." The tears finally left their place beneath her eyelids and silently steamed down her face. The crystal heart held her gaze throughout the torrent of emotions - love, fear, regret, and finally, a deep calm which settled in her own heart. She sat watching, lost in her feelings, until the sun had set below the buildings beyond her.

She rose from the wicker chair to go back inside. Upon standing, a final fit of coughing possessed her, tearing through her body like never before. Unable to catch herself, she fell to the floor. This time she did not bother to raise the handkerchief to her lips; there was something more important to clutch in her hand. Fingering the links on the necklace as if counting the Rosary, her soul sighed from her now useless body with a single ahh-men. Tony found her the next morning, with Babe perched vigilantly atop her head, standing guard over his friend.

Four days later, Benjamin returned home from the funeral, feeling miserable. His shirt collar was too tight, his suit itched and faintly smelled of mothballs, but his misery was more than mere discomfort. A hole had been ripped open in his life that he feared would never be filled.

Maddie's daughter, Leslie, had been wonderful. In fact, her whole family had been more consoling to him than he to them. Maddie had apparently been singing his praises for years, and despite the circumstances, her family was glad to finally meet him. When Leslie found out that the crystal heart her mother had died holding (so tightly that it had to be pried out of her fist) was his last present to her, she insisted Maddie be buried with it. This act had touched Benjamin deeply.

In Maddie's will, she had left Benjamin Angel,

Gabriel, and Cherub. He also was given her fountain pen and the inlaid wooden box which contained all of his letters to her. Benjamin treasured the correspondence and pen more than he would have his weight in gold. He reverently placed them beside the ancient cigar boxes which held every note she had ever sent him. He opened the pigeon cases he was carrying, returning Babe and the other three to the coop. Tony had been given the remaining two: Michael and Raphael.

Dazed, he half-heartedly leafed through the book on Baseball Greats. Part-way through it, he slowly let it slip from his fingers to his lap and, for the better part of an hour, he just stared into space. With an almost invisible movement, his chest began to shiver with each inhalation. Each quivering breath began to progress into a noticeable tremble, until a sob finally escaped from his lips, followed by a soul-wrenching weeping.

"I never told her; I never got to tell her," he kept repeating. Over and over, this litany continued as the weight of his loss settled heavier upon him. The only time that they ever were face to face was, not when he planned to declare his love, but at her viewing at the funeral parlor. He knew the serenity she wore on her face was not the result of a skillful embalmer, but rather the natural view she had presented to the world. He had longed to stroke her soft hair, to have her open her eyes and beg her to forgive him for being too late - for he could never forgive himself. No absolution for this Lutheran, he grimly thought.

This cycle of sadness and shame was broken by the flutter of wings on his fire escape. Looking up, he saw an unfamiliar pigeon rapidly strutting back and forth in front of the window, acting as if it desperately wanted to come inside.

With curiosity overriding his grief, Benjamin opened the window. The white and gray bird flew to the kitchen, landed on the table, and proceeded to make herself at home.

"Well, who are you?" he asked, as if expecting an answer. Receiving no reply, he moved closer to examine the bird. He then noticed a note was attached to one of her legs. He had no idea who had trained this bird to deliver a message; he thought that he knew most of the pigeon trainers in Boston. She was unusual looking enough that he would have recognized seeing her in anyone else's coop.

Although he hadn't checked the pigeon's sex yet, its broad pelvis said "brooder," and its appearance just gave the impression of a female. She was almost pure white, without the green patina that many of the pigeons possess on their heads and necks. The Quaker gray areas were small, and appeared to be placed randomly over her body. Now that she was inside, she had grown calm, and her bright eyes were taking in the apartment... and him. He felt almost uncomfortable in her gaze.

Still, years of habit overruled his illogical reaction, and he removed the message. Shock quickly set in as he read the fountain penned words.

Benjamin:

I regret we won't be able to meet as you planned. I want to thank you for the heart - it is absolutely lovely. You must know that I shall treasure it for all eternity. Don't hole yourself up in that apartment of yours. Go make peace with John and his family. Remember, youngster - life is too short.

I must close.

With all my love,
Maddie

P.S. And dear Benjamin, don't worry - I know.

"She knew!" Benjamin moaned in wonder. Strength left his legs and he gracelessly plopped onto the couch, the first smile in days daring to cross his time-creased face. Then logic reared its ugly head and began spewing out some disquieting questions.

How the bird and letter got to him could reasonably be explained: Tony or one of Maddie's family probably just found the note and sent it. Other questions did not answer themselves so easily; two in particular: how could she have written regarding canceling their meeting; and how would she know about the heart unless she wrote just minutes before dying; and... when did she obtain and train this bird? He looked at his guest, searching for answers.

The bird quietly returned his stare, unblinking. After what seemed to be an eternity, the pigeon began to preen herself, fluffing and separating each feather. As she circled in cleaning her back, she raised high her wing closest to Benjamin and again, he faced something wondrous.

Under a bird's wing there is an area, the "armpit" if you will, where the skin shows through and there is little down and no feathers. On her pink flesh was a white heart-shaped birthmark, no mistake. Benjamin clearly could see its sharp outline. However, it was the gray splayed V of a bird's silhouette in the center of this birthmark that caused him to tremble and cry out with fearful longing..."Maddie?"

URBAN FLIGHT

Benjamin gave a sigh of nervous relief as he released his newest pigeon into the skies. It had taken him two days to get his courage up to share this event with someone - Tony was the only person that he felt could even entertain the possibility of what Benjamin was imagining without trying to lock him up as insane. At least, Ben prayed, that Tony would not find him nuts.

If this bird will take the note to Tony, that is, Benjamin thought. He had taken the chance that the bird knew how to get to Tony's balcony as well as she knew where Maddie's coop was. The young man was right beside Maddie's apartment, so the odds were good that the message as well as the messenger would be received.

So he turned and went inside, with crossed fingers and held breath.

Tony,
    I can only assume you will be the one getting this. I have no logical basis for my conclusion but I sense that this bird will find her way home to roast in your coop.
    (If I am wrong, whoever gets this message kindly write me back and explain your ownership of this bird. Thank you.)
    Anyway, Tony, I enjoyed meeting you at the wake, even if it was under such devastating circumstances. I will always regret missing her by such a few hours. I will never forgive myself for being such an old fool in waiting to see her.
    I missed you at the funeral. Her family was very kind to me. It was a beautiful ceremony. Maddie would have liked it. Going there was the hardest thing I have ever had to do.
    When I got home, this beauty arrived. From

where, I do not know. I named her Maddie or maybe she named herself? Under her left wing there is a strange mark that looks just like the crystal heart I gave Maddie. You don't think... No, just the foolish hopings of an old man.

God, I miss her!

Hope your classes are going well. I look forward to your reply.

Benjamin

Benjamin,

How are you holding up? If you need anything, don't hesitate to ask. Maddie asked me to keep an eye on you the day before she died - to keep you out of trouble, that kind of thing. Sorry I could not make the funeral. I will be going to the cemetery late this afternoon.

I have no idea where the bird came from. Wild about the birthmark, though. Pretty amazing coincidence.

School is going well.

I miss her too.

Tony

Fighting back tears, Tony laid the flowers on Maddie's headstone. Folding his hands together, he bowed his head and said a silent prayer. Behind him the sun had begun its evening descent. A single teardrop escaped his left eye and slid down his face. Wiping it away, he spoke softly to his departed friend.

"Hi, Maddie. It's me, Tony. Sorry I didn't make the funeral. I had a law mid-term that I couldn't get out of. I couldn't even weasel out of a lousy test. Some lawyer I'll make, huh?"

"I can hear you now telling me I will make a fine attorney. You said it so many times before, it is probably just echoing from somewhere far away. I just hope you are right. I aced the test and made the law review: I am now seventh in my class. Last time we spoke, I was only eighth." He hesitated, then continued . "I would give it all up to get you back, Maddie. You were the last family I had."

"Your angels are doing well. Benjamin has the ones you left him plus a new one. Homes in on both my coop and his. Named it Maddie, after you. We have no clue where it came from. Poor old guy misses you something fierce. He has it bad for you."

"I don't blame him - you were a special lady. I miss you. Your death still does not seem real. I feel like I will walk down to your apartment and find you there. Or you will just come up behind me and tap me on the shoulder and say, 'Just kidding!' "

As if on cue, Tony felt an unexpected quick jolt on his own back. Caught unaware, he vaulted into the air, screaming. As soon as he touched down, he dove behind the headstone and waited for his heart to restart.

It was not a ghost that had frightened him close to death, but a panting golden retriever. The friendly dog's tongue hung slightly out of his mouth and his bright eyes seemed to be laughing at Tony's reaction. Tony was more than able to take a joke and put out the palm of his hand for the canine to smell before he attempted to pet him.

"You scared the crap out of me, boy! Don't sneak up on people in a graveyard like that," Tony said, reaching to scratch behind the golden retriever's ears. The dog liked it so much he let Tony continue. "You are a good boy, aren't you? Where is your owner? Are you out here all by yourself?" The dog did not answer except to start running back and forth. "You want to play, do you?" The dog kept running, which Tony assumed was a yes.

He picked up a stick and threw it across the rows of graves. In the distance, a group of junior high school boys were playing touch football. The dog ran after the stick and brought it back to Tony but did not want to give it up easily. The dog insisted Tony play tug of war for it. Tony won and threw the stick again. The dog chased merrily after it and again returned it. This time the tug of war was more serious and the dog made it clear he had been nice enough the first time to let Tony win. Tony pulled with both hands as the dog shook his head side to side.

"You are too good for me. Guess I'll have to give up," Tony said, letting go of the stick. The dog looked up at him as though he was crazy, asking with his expression 'Why did you stop playing?' Tony replied with a laugh. "You have to give it to me or I won't play." The dog looked him over and put the stick in his hands to try to encourage Tony to participate. When that did not work, the dog begrudgingly dropped the stick.

Tony picked it up and threw it again, this time in the opposite direction. The dog chased after it. Too late, Tony saw the open grave. He instinctively yelled "Look out!" to the dog who, instead of stopping, kept running with his head turned back to look at Tony. The golden retriever fell right into the open pit.

"Uh-oh!" said Tony, running over to the edge of the hole. He was relieved to see the dog standing at the bottom, stick in his mouth and wagging his tail, unhurt.

"How are we going to get you out of there?" Tony asked. The golden retriever continued wagging and panting. "I can see you are going to be a huge help. I can't lift you out by your collar. That would strangle you. Maybe if I climb down, I can lift you out."

Tony lay face down on the ground and began to lower his legs over the edge. Slowly, he inched his way down until his stomach was holding his legs over the drop. He tried to move the rest of the way gradually, but gravity had other plans. His right hand slipped on the dew- moistened grass and the left hand lost its grip entirely. Tony started sliding, desperately trying to regain a hand hold. He picked up speed and fell unceremoniously, landing on his buttocks.

Laying flat on his back, he looked up at the sky, which was now several feet further away than it was moments before. Tony closed his eyes and said "Great! I suppose things could be worse."

The golden retriever took this as an invitation to lick his face.

"You did not have to prove my point," Tony said, trying not to drown in dog saliva. The retriever picked up the stick and dropped it in Tony's lap. "At least you do not hold a grudge, but in case you have not noticed, there is no room to throw in here," The look on the dog's face remained unchanged. "Fine. Go fetch," Tony said, tossing the stick three feet. "Now, how do we get out of here? It seemed so easy a minute ago, but it's much deeper in here than standing up there."

Tony reached up to grip the earth walls and tried to pull himself up by wedging his hands and feet in the dirt. He got about a foot up before the soil gave way and he came crashing down. Tony tried again and succeed only in pulling down more silt. The golden retriever thought it was a new game and started digging up the grave floor with his two front paws.

"Good idea. I'll try to go up and over; you dig toward China. First one out send back help," Tony said, still trying to scale the sides. Finally, in frustration, he admitted defeat. "This is useless; we need a ladder."

Tony sat down on the dirt floor. The retriever laid his head in Tony's lap, silently demanding to be petted.

"I guess I have no choice but to swallow my pride and yell for help...Help! I've fallen and I can't get out!" Tony yelled. No one answered, so he screamed some more. The golden retriever stared at him strangely, but decided this was yet another game and started howling. As the dog was louder than Tony, he shrugged his shoulders, saying "If you can't beat them, join them." Tony started howling, adding his efforts to those of the dog, who was enjoying the canine sing-a-long immensely

In the distance, a third, human voice joined the chorus, howling as if in answer to the call. It became louder.

"It's working!" Tony said to the dog. "Keep doing it! Either we are about to be rescued or we're going to have another player for fetch."

The retriever responded with silence. Tony shook his head in exasperation and continued howling on his own.

Footsteps were heard and a voice cried out, "Zeus! Is that you?"

The golden retriever started barking wildly, running in circles. "Yep, sure is. Down here," Tony said.

"That's funny, Zeus. You only barked before," a woman said, coming to stand over the precipice. The golden retriever barked with more passion.

"Young dogs can learn new tricks. What do you think?"

"That would be more impressive if I couldn't see the dog's lips move. You mind explaining who you are and what are you doing with my dog in an open grave?"

"Zeus here started to dig a hole to bury a bone. I told

him it was too big, but one thing lead to another, and here we are."

"That's not funny. I'm not amused."

"You should be. This is a funny situation," Tony grinned. The woman merely stared down icily at him. "Well, truth be told, I was visiting the grave of a friend and Zeus scared the heck out of me."

"So you threw him in the grave?"

"Hardly. Actually, we started playing fetch and Zeus fell in. I tried to warn him, but he kept right on running."

"That sounds like Zeus... lovable, but dumb. How did you get down there?"

"I was trying to get him out and I kind of fell in."

"Pretty boneheaded."

"Absolutely, but from here I have really gotten a new perspective."

"Ahh... Zen and the freshly dug Grave."

"Exactly."

"Have you had enough perspective yet?"

"Absolutely."

"Good. then the next point of business is - how do we get the two of you out of there?"

"Wait! How do I know you are Zeus's rightful owner?"

"Who else would want him?" the woman said. Zeus looked up, half hurt as if he understood what was said.

"Could I see some ID?" Tony said with mock seriousness.

"Look at the collar; it says 'Zeus' and to contact Jennifer Robbins if he is lost."

Tony looked at the tag. "That is what it says, all right. Nice to make your acquaintance, Jennifer."

"Charmed. You have a name?"

"Nope. Usually, I answer to 'Hey, you'."

"Chinese, is it?"

"Mongolian."

"So, I should call you 'Hey, you'?"

"Well, my friends call me Tony Jordan. Kind of a nickname."

"Okay then, Tony, how should I go about rescuing the gentleman in distress?"

"Well, I'm not in distress, actually."

"If you want me to leave you there, I could."

"If it would make you feel better to rescue me, I could hardly take that away from you, now could I?"

"What a kind man you are."

"Too true. Any ropes or ladders up there?"

"None that I can see."

"Well, how about we get Zeus out first, then the two of you can go look for something to get me out. I could lift him up to where you could pull him the rest of the way."

The woman crossed her arms and, with a twinkle in her eyes, asked, "How do you know we just won't take off and leave you stranded?"

"People who care about animals are generally good folks; besides it's not like I have any choice."

"Sounds like a plan."

Tony bent and picked up Zeus. The dog responded by trying to lick his face. "Easy, Zeus," he said. "You ready up there?"

"Yep. Lift him up slowly," Jennifer said, her torso leaning over the edge and her arms reaching down.

"I am. Just be careful. It is slippery up there."

"I can take care of myself. I'm not the one who fell in," Jennifer said, grabbing onto Zeus below the dog's shoulders. "Got him," Jennifer said. Zeus started kicking all four legs, trying to get a foot hold on the dirt wall. "Stop fidgeting, pumpkin. I don't want to drop you."

Zeus listened somewhat as Jennifer reverse-commando crawled, using twists of her hips and legs to move. As Zeus got to the top, he started to squirm again, causing Jennifer to almost lose her grip. "He's slipping!" she yelled.

"If he falls, I will try to catch him," Tony said from inside the hole.

Jennifer lunged forward on her stomach so as not to lose her grip. Her body was now parallel with the grave. Rolling, she pulled the golden retriever out with one great tug and he was free. Unfortunately for her, for every reaction there was an equal and opposite reaction: the effort of pulling the dog free pushed her just over the edge. Tony's arms broke her fall, but not without knocking the breath out of him as they both tumbled to the ground.

"Zeus, you've gained some weight," Tony gasped.

"I'm sorry!" Jennifer exclaimed, helping Tony to his feet and trying to brush the dirt off him. "Are you all right?"

"I'm fine," he waved her off.

"Good." She stared up at the hole's edge. "I can't believe I fell in."

"Pretty boneheaded," Tony joked.

Jennifer laughed. "I guess I deserved that. I thought graves were only supposed to be six feet deep. This must be nine or ten."

"Obviously someone was enthusiastic about their work," Tony said. "What do we do now?"

"I could climb onto your shoulders and you could try to lift me out. Then I could find a ladder for you."

"Let's try it."

Tony bent down on one knee and Jennifer climbed on his shoulders. Unsteadily, he stood.

"You're a lot heavier than Zeus."

"Don't you know you're not supposed to make disparaging comments about a woman's weight?"

"Usually I don't, but most women don't ask for rides on my back. Shall I guess your age now?"

"Go ahead. Most women are not sensitive about that until after thirty. Just for future reference, you should guess low on both."

"The weight I won't even try, although maybe you should try lifting me."

"Hey!" Jennifer said, tapping Tony's head gently but with authority.

"Just kidding. You are very thin. I'm sure I must have had this hernia before and just never noticed it. I should be thanking you for bring it to my attention. Can you reach the top?"

"Barely touching. Maybe if I stood on your shoulders."

"Normally I do not let people walk all over me like this, but in your case I will make an exception."

"Thanks. So how old do you think I am?"

"Twenty two?"

"Close. Twenty four. Okay, my hands are on the top."

"Stand up all the way and I will push your feet."

Stood she did and push she did, but Jennifer's upper body was not strong enough to pull her up the rest of the way. To top it all off, she slipped again on the dewy grass and plummeted.

"Fall down and go boom?" asked Tony.

"Real cute. Let's try it again."

They did with no more success other than getting her head and one shoulder up and out before Zeus licked her face and she fell again.

"That is not going to work. Any other ideas?" asked Jennifer.

"We could get Zeus to go for help."

"You mean like Lassie?"

"Exactly," Tony said, looking up at Zeus who had squatted down on his belly to better look down the hole.

"You don't know Zeus."

"Still worth a try. C'mon boy, go get help," Tony said. The dog remained motionless. "Go on. Fetch the care-taker, a cop, a girl scout selling cookies, anybody."

Zeus tilted his head to the side and looked back at Tony.

"It's not working, is it?" asked Tony.

"Nope. Maybe if you tell him Timmy fell down a well and is about to be eaten by sharks," Jennifer offered. Tony did as she suggested. Zeus stood and ran off.

"He understood!"

"I don't think so. Look," said Jennifer, pointing above them. Zeus had returned with a stick in his mouth, which he dropped on Tony's head. "I guess I might as well get used to being stuck here."

"It's not so bad, once you get used to it," said Tony.

"Really?"

"No, not really. Just trying to help. Did it work?"

"Actually, it did a little. I appreciate you trying to help Zeus. Thanks."

"My pleasure. Wish I was more successful."

"Me too," Jennifer said turning to face Tony. Their faces were inches away and the physical proximity created a sudden intimacy that neither was quite prepared for. Each took a step back and a moment of awkward silence ensued.

Tony broke the stillness first. "Come here often?"

"Nope. First time. Yourself?"

"I'm a newcomer, too. Heard it really knocked them dead."

"With a joke like that it is understandable."

Above them, the sky had turned a deep red as the sun continued its downward trek.

"What are you doing hanging out in a graveyard?"

"Walking the dog. Only place in the area with enough room to let him run free. Tonight he ran a little too free, too fast, and I lost him."

"I found him or rather he found me. Scared me half to death."

"What were you doing here?"

"Paying my respects to a special lady."

"Your wife?"

"No, a friend. More of a grandmother really."

"You were close?"

"Very."

"I'm sorry for your loss. What was her name?"

"Maddie Logan."

"How did she die? Was it sudden?"

"Yes and no. We knew she was dying, but we thought she had longer. She had TADS."

"I've been hearing about that in the news. Horrible, kills your immune system. Why didn't she go into one of those bubbles?"

"She did not want to become an Innuendo. Maddie refused to give up her life. She had always lived on her own terms and she choose to die the same way."

"I can almost understand why; living in one of those bubbles would be awful. Never to be able to go outside again, never to feel sunlight on your face again. Dying would almost be better."

"I would argue with you on that one. Where there is life, there is hope. Had Maddie gone in she might still be alive. Miserable, but alive. She would never have given up her angels."

"Figurines?"

"No, homing pigeons. Called them angels, named them after angels too."

"Sounds like an interesting lady. How did you meet her?"

"We, my parents and I, lived in that apartment building since I was a kid. She was always just a nice lady to me, taught me about birds. When I was a senior in high school, my parents were killed by a drunk driver; I was devastated. Since I was still a minor, Social Services tried to step in. They wanted to put me in a foster home and sell off the condo apartment which my parents had left to me. I had no relatives to stick up for me, but Maddie stepped in and told them she was my grandaunt on my mother's side and demanded that I stay with her. They did not believe her, but she hired a lawyer and stalled things long enough for me to reach my eighteenth birthday. Then, I was a legal adult and they could not touch me."

"So you lived with her?"

"Only for a few weeks. When I was ready, she let me move back into my apartment. Installed an intercom system so I would not be alone. Fed me dinner and made my lunch every day until I graduated. She even helped me invest the money from my parents' life insurance policy so the mortgage on the condo unit was paid and there was enough left over for college. Seeing what she was able to do with a lawyer to help me helped me decide what I wanted to do with my life."

"You became a lawyer."

"Almost," he corrected. "A few more semesters, the bar exam, and I will be there. I want to set up shop working for the underdog, folks who the system would walk all over otherwise."

"Do-gooders don't make much money." She said with a wink, "I thought lawyers were in it for the money."

"Not all attorneys want to be ambulance chasers. I don't need much money. No rent to pay helps keep the bills down."

"I guess it would," Jennifer giggled at their situation. "You know, it seems so normal, sitting down here talking to you."

"What could be more natural?"

"For all I know, you could be some psycho killer."

Tony rolled his eyes and smiled evilly. "You are right; this is all a plot."

"Well," she quipped. "It is somebody's plot."

"Ouch! You said my jokes were bad... that pun was horrible."

"Best kind."

The view of the sky above them was taking on a dusky

hue, and the evening's coolness began to wash gently down on them, causing them to shyly draw close to one another.

"You getting cold?" Tony asked, as he offered her his coat in a gentlemanly manner. She shook her head no, but continued to maintain her position of nearness.

"These aren't called sweats for nothing!" she said with a grin and a mock waving of her hand as if to cool herself.

"Well, if you change your mind, this jacket of mine makes a great blanket."

Muffled shouts and laughter came from above, beyond the grave. They could hear voices in all the between stages of boys to men: deep, hoarse, and cracking high in their collective excitement of an evening out, playing tag football and hanging together.

"We're saved, we're saved!" Tony yelled, grabbing Jennifer's shoulders and tossing her up and down until they were both jumping like a couple of rescued castaways. Zeus, who had been watching the festivities from above, began to jump about himself, adding to the merriment.

"Go get 'em, boy!" Jennifer urged the beast. "Bring them here." But Zeus just continued to wiggle and whine.

As the dog stared down in confusion, Tony got a bright idea and shook the stick Zeus had given him earlier. "Come on, boy. Go get the stick."

Zeus joyfully leapt out of sight after the stick, which Tony had heaved in the direction of the voices. "Between Zeus and us yelling, they are bound to come over," he said with confidence.

"Hey, look at the dog... here, boy!" One of the teens was trying to coax Zeus over to him. Several others could be heard whistling to the lumbering dog. Tony and Jennifer began to shout "Help us, help!"

"What was that?" one of the group whispered.

"OK, guys... whose playing us for fools? Quit trying to

scare us."

The trapped pair increased their cries. "Help! We're trapped here! Get us out!"

One boy was doing a fair imitation of the Cowardly Lion. "I do believe in spooks, I do believe in spooks, I do, I do , I do!" he croaked in a whisper.

Tony took a deep breath and bellowed, "COME HERE, DAMN IT!"

Instead of the boys coming to help, this announcement only drove them away.

"Oh Lord, ...ghosts!" one squealed, his former baritone suddenly turned falsetto. Scuffling frantically, the football team dropped their ball and made like a track team, each one of them going for the gold. A moment later, Zeus happily returned to the pit, football tucked between his huge jaws. He dropped-licked it to his mistress, and waited for her return pass.

Jennifer looked down at the spittle-covered ball and then at Tony. "Oh, well... we might as well get comfortable. It looks as if we're here for the night."

"Look at it this way..." Tony said. "How many people in Boston get to sleep out under the stars nowadays without the fear of getting mugged?" The two of them laughed over that one. "Between Zeus here and the terror of the cemetery residents, we are probably in the safest place in town."

"I've been complaining that my life has been too boring lately..." Jennifer giggled, rolling her eyes. "I guess this qualifies as a change of pace."

"That's me, lady...Mr. Excitement!" Tony boasted with a grin.

They sat down together and began to search the skies for the first star to wish on.

Tony glanced over at his pitmate and thought to himself, "This night is probably going to be one of the shortest in my life; I am definitely going to ask her out in the morning...but how am I going to top this?" He started, as he felt her hand lightly land on his, and the both of them laughed as they simultaneously sighed. "Yep," he agreed with himself, "a very short night."

It was like waking in a cave, a cave with a sunroof, Jeni mused. Tony was asleep on her shoulder, her arm around his shoulder, his arm draped across her stomach. She remembered Tony falling asleep but not herself. Looking up she saw Zeus, asleep but still at his post, guarding over their grave.

Jeni thought she should be exhausted. They had talked almost the entire night away, stopping only when exhaustion overcame them. Having spent the night with little or no sleep, sitting on cold earth, Jeni expected to feel stiff and awkward. Instead, she woke refreshed, feeling wonderful, almost giddy. It had been the most wonderful night she could remember. Never before had she bared so much of her soul to anyone in such comfort. She had only known Tony hours, but already he seemed like a friend she had known for a lifetime.

Looking down at his sleeping face, she felt a warmth envelope her, feelings of tenderness and protectiveness overwhelmed her. Jeni bent to kiss him on top of his head and hugged him tight. Still asleep, he hugged her back. Looking at her watch, she realized she was already late for class and decided she would rather be nowhere else than here. Jeni had never missed class before, never even cut. Given a choice between a lecture and letting Tony sleep, Tony won. Jeni was amazed at herself for this decision. School had always come first in her life. Sure she dated, but she never allowed anyone to distract her from her goals. This seemed different somehow.

Part of her realized she was being insane. She did not

know this man; who knew how they would interact outside of a hole in the ground? The part that was now in control felt entirely opposite. Never one to gamble on anything bigger than a lottery ticket, she realized she had already anted up on the biggest bet of her life. The stakes were nothing less than her heart. Jeni knew love was no fairy tale. Relationships were hard work. If she won, happiness might be hers. If she lost, it would be a guarantee of nothing less than total heartbreak. To her, it was worth the risk.

Jeni hugged him tight again. As she listened, the morning breeze carried the sounds of a whistled song to her ears. The song was indistinguishable, as it was comprised of only three notes with no discernible beat.

"Zeus," Jeni shouted, waking the sleeping dog. "Go fetch!" Jeni threw the stick Zeus had dropped in the grave the night before, knowing full well he would run to give it to anyone in the area.

"Tony, wake up," Jeni said softly, gently rubbing his head. "Someone is coming. We can get out."

It took a minute for Tony to register where he was and the significance of what Jeni said.

"Morning," Tony mumbled, stretching the cobwebs and kinks out of his stiff muscles. "I guess it is time to get up and out, huh?"

"Looks that way. Shall we try the shouting method again?"

"Yep."

Together they yelled, "Help!" This caused Zeus to run back to the top of the grave.

A diminutive, lanky man followed behind the dog, holding the stick. He had a receding hair line of curly red locks and a bushy mustache.

"What the blazes are you two doing down there? This ain't no love motel. Damn kinky freaks!" the man said.

"It's nothing like that," Jeni said, indignantly. "My

dog fell in this open grave."

"Don't look that way to me," the man replied.

"Of course not. We got him out, we just could not get ourselves out," said Tony.

"I 'm going to have to call the police, you know."

"What for?" asked Tony incredulously.

"Trespassing, of course."

"You don't have to do that, do you?" asked Jeni.

"Absolutely," said the little man, obviously reveling in the little bit of power fate had dropped in his lap. "Unless, of course, you gave me some cash to look the other way."

"You want us to bribe you?" Jeni asked, aghast.

"More of a gift, really," the little man replied smugly.

"Why you..." Jeni started.

Tony interrupted with a calming hand on her shoulder. "May I?" he asked, with a wink. Jeni smiled and nodded. "We actually want you to call the police, so go ahead."

"You want me to call the cops?" the man repeated, momentarily thrown off his stride.

"Absolutely. That way we can add false arrest to the list of charges against the cemetery."

"Charges?"

"For the lawsuit. Hard to dispute an arrest report."

"What are you, a lawyer?" the man said sarcastically.

"As a matter of fact, yes," Tony replied.

"You were still trespassing, which is a crime," the man shot back.

"We were here during visiting hours, visiting the grave of a friend of mine who had passed away last week."

"Prove it."

"Her death is a matter of public record. To top that off, there was no barricade or warning signs around this open pit to warn off people. Very sloppy; I must assume you are the caretaker?" Tony asked.

"Yes," replied the man warily.

"So it was your responsibility to post the signs and

check to make sure the cemetery was empty before going home for the night. Then, this morning when you finally do find us, you harass us with threats and coercion instead of getting us out of here as quickly as possible. Rest assured, you will be named in the suit. And what is your name?" Tony ordered, attempting to give the impression of towering height while standing several feet below the caretaker. The verbal and physical posturing was paying off; the man was looking visibly shaken.

"Roy Maser," the man stammered.

"Roy Maser... we'll note that for the legal papers. We also both injured our backs and necks falling in. These injuries were aggravated by spending the night in a cold damp environment. May require years of therapy, not to mention the mental anguish."

"Mental anguish?"

"From spending the night in a cemetery. Jeni here was terrified."

"I was?" Jeni asked. Tony gently elbowed her. "Oh, I was. Every noise I heard I thought was one of the undead trying to get to us to devour our brains. I'm still shaking." She shuddered for effect.

"I could just bury you both, you know," Roy said, trying to be sinister and failing. The sounds of a gravesite service could be heard just a short distance away.

"And Zeus would rip out your throat," Jeni said. "Plus you could not stop me from screaming. Watch." Jeni let out a prolonged blood-curdling scream that actually halted the nearby service.

"Okay, okay. I will go get a ladder. I think there is one in the tool shed," Roy said frantically, mumbling to himself as he walked off.

"Pretty impressive, Mr. Lawyer. A little lie there?" Jeni said with a smile.

"By the time the case actually got to court it would be true. Very impressive lung capacity, there. Every consider a career in B movies?"

"Nah! I would never be dumb enough to stay in high heels when a monster is chasing me."

"And that story about Zeus ripping his throat out...Nice touch."

"Zeus may not be the smartest dog in the world, but he is very protective. He would not let anyone hurt me."

"Neither would I," Tony promised solemnly.

"Ditto," said Jeni, putting her hand on Tony's arm. Neither made a sound as they gazed at one another. Turning to face each other fully, their lips came together almost hesitantly. In tenderness and passion, like every love story told, the rest of the world faded from existence... for a time.

The sound of a metal ladder clanking above failed to rouse them from each other, so finally Roy had to resort to verbal tactics.

"Break it up!" Roy growled in disgust several times before the pair parted to look up at him. "The owner of this site has shown up early. The mourners are already walking over here, so hurry up and get out of there."

Roy slid the ladder down to them. The mourners, dressed in black and weeping, were only a few yards from the grave. Roy saw them and said, "Oh, crap!" He quickly ran to look busy pulling weeds around a nearby tombstone.

"Where did he go?" asked Tony.

"Who cares? Lets get out of here," answered Jeni.

"After you," Tony said, bowing with a flourish.

Tony held the ladder as Jeni climbed out. The mourners had reached the graveside and stood stunned as they watched a woman climb out. Jeni saw them and smiled weakly, then turned to hold the top of the ladder for Tony. As his head cleared the top, Jeni whispered to him "We're not alone."

"Where were they last night when we needed them?"

Tony whispered back. Jeni giggled. "What do we tell them?"

"I know," Jeni said. She turned to their audience and announced. "Grave inspectors; just a last minute check, folks."

"Sorry for your loss," Tony added. "But you can rest easy that the grave is in tip top condition."

The mourners looked around at each other confused. One actually said "Thank you." As Jeni and Tony turned to go, they saw Roy behind a neighboring tombstone looking as if he was about to pull out what was left of his hair.

"Do you think we should pull the ladder out for him?" asked Jeni.

"Why? He did not do any favors for us." Tony said with a half laugh. Zeus ran up to Jeni demanding to be petted. She obliged. Tony reached for her free hand and began leading her off.

"Where are we going?" Jeni asked.

"You'll see," Tony replied as he walked a few rows over to a familiar gravesite.

"This is Maddie's grave?" Jeni asked when they stopped there.

"Yes," Tony answered with his head bowed. Jeni squeezed his hand. Neither one let go. "This may be a little weird, but it seemed appropriate. I wanted to bring you here, kind of introduce you. Jeni, this is Maddie," Turning to the temporary tombstone, he said "Maddie, this is Jeni."

"Pleasure to meet you, Maddie," Jeni said.

Tony bent down to pick up the bouquet of flowers he had left the night before and plucked a rose out. He handed it to Jeni. "This is for you."

"Thanks. Are you sure it's okay?"

"Maddie would not have minded; she was constantly trying to fix me up. She would tell me flowers are wasted on the dead and to give you the whole bunch. To tell the truth, I would not be surprised if she somehow set this whole thing up."

Jeni kissed him on the cheek. "Busy for the rest of the day?"

"Yes," Tony said. Jeni's face dropped. "Spending it with you," he winked.

Pure joy washed both their faces clean of the night's strains.

"Walk me home?" Jeni asked.

"My pleasure," Tony said, enfolding Jeni in his arms and being enveloped in hers in turn. Zeus ran side to side while following them, then stopped to stare at a pigeon that had landed atop the tombstone. It was white, with speckles of gray. Zeus went to sniff the bird, then stopped and barked once. The bird's feathers were unruffled. Not knowing what else to do, the dog chased back after Jeni and Tony.

The bird stayed perched on the tombstone, staring at the couple and bobbing her head contentedly.

Benjamin,

The most amazing thing happened. I went to the cemetery to visit Maddie and I fell in a grave. Well, actually, a dog fell in. Then I fell in trying to get him out. Then this woman, the dog's owner, helps me get the dog out, but falls in herself. We did not get out until morning. We talked the entire night away. It was the most amazing night.

Her name is Jeni and I have gone out with her every night this week. She is beautiful, smart, and funny. I think I am in love. I am meeting her in twenty minutes so I have to run.

How is everything with you?

Take care.

Tony

Tony,

Congratulations on meeting the young lady. She sounds quite nice. Let me make sure I understand you correctly - you met her in a graveyard? Is that one of the hot new pick up spots? Last I heard, the supermarket was the place to go, but I might be a little out of touch.

Back in my day we went to dance halls. Times change.

I am enjoying Maddie's company immensely.

Be well.

Benjamin

BIRDS OF A FEATHER

one year later

Benjamin swiftly walked to answer the expected knock on his door, even if it was twenty minutes past due.

"Hello," said Benjamin. "You must be Jeni."

"Yes I am, which means you must be Benjamin," Jeni said, shaking the out-stretched hand.

"Yes, I must be. No choice in the matter. No one else wants the job. Please come in. Can I get you anything?"

"Soda?"

"Coming up. Please have a seat."

"Tony led me to believe you are a messy housekeeper. This place is cleaner than his," Jeni said, lowering herself onto the couch.

"Truth be told, I am a slob but I straighten for company," Benjamin said, handing her the drink. "So, Tony tells me you are interested in pigeons."

"Kind of. They are a hobby of his, so I want to learn, but sometimes being too close to a teacher can be detrimental to the learning process. Besides, I think he wants me to see that someone else besides him is into this."

"Well, why don't we start by introducing you to the kids," Benjamin said, standing and leading the way to the coop. Pointing to each individually, he told their names. "This is Babe, Dizzy Dean, Micky, and Joe. They were all raised and trained by me."

"Named them after baseball players?"

"Each and every one. This next group is Angel, Gabriel, and Cherub. They were raised by my friend Maddie, as were Tony's Wings and Michael."

"So they can find their way home from anywhere on earth."

"I don't know. The furthest my kids have ever gone is from New York to here. Brought them down whenever I went to see a Yankee game. They have to be trained by gradually increasing the distance, although a pigeon the army trained once found its way home by traveling twenty three hundred miles."

"How long have homing pigeons been around?"

"Five thousand years, give or take a couple."

"You're kidding?"

"Nope. They carried news of the Olympics in ancient Greece. But you did not come all the way down here to hear an old man ramble on about birds."

"Why else would I be here?"

"You tell me."

"I am not sure what you are trying to say."

"Forget it. Would you like to feed one of them?"

"Sure," Jeni said. Benjamin pulled out Maddie. "What is this one's name?" she asked.

"Maddie."

"You named her after your friend?

"Not exactly. She kind of came with the name already attached."

"What do you mean?"

"Much too complicated to explain. Here, put the feed into your palm like this," Benjamin said. When Maddie bobbed down to peck, Jeni jerked away her hand, startling the bird. "Relax, she won't hurt you. That's it. Haven't you ever fed Tony's birds?"

"Yes, but he puts the seeds in a tray."

"That's the way to do it for everyday meals. For bonding, it should be done by hand. Helps them get to know and trust you."

Maddie pecked again, but Jeni did not flinch. Before long she was an old pro. Jeni made causal conversation. The weather. Politics. What was going on this week around town.

"Tony told me about how Maddie just showed up at your window one day and knew to fly between your coop and his, without being trained. Unusual, isn't it?"

"Impossible, but there she is."

"Didn't you search for an answer?"

"At first, until I realized the answer was right under

my nose."

"What was it?"

"Just as it was right under my nose, so it is under yours."

She gingerly touched her upper lip, then shrugged. "Nope, nothing there, I'm afraid."

They both laughed.

"Did you know Maddie long?"

"Years. She is a very dear friend," Benjamin said. Jeni noted, but did not correct his use of the present tense. "I just wish I had met her before her death."

"So you never actually met her?" Jeni asked.

"No. Not in person, only in pigeon," Benjamin said, chuckling at his own joke. "But we met each other, knew each other, dare I say, loved each other, through our words. On paper, we were able to create ourselves anew, could have made ourselves perfect, but choose not to. We showed our true hearts and souls and shared them shamelessly."

"Sounds very romantic."

"I never thought of it that way. Maddie was my friend, near and dear," Benjamin said, glancing at the pigeon.

"You lived so close. Why did you not meet sooner?"

"Never needed to. Our relationship was full."

"Why ruin a good thing?"

"Basically, but there was more to it. Maybe part of it was fear. Maddie knew me, warts and all. It did not matter to her. Still, I am a rather crotchety old man."

"You seem rather charming to me."

"You flatter me. I am not used to compliments from beautiful young women. Anyone, even myself, can be charming for an hour, days even, but eventually the facade fades. Maybe if Maddie actually saw how big my warts were, things would have changed."

"Or perhaps she would have kissed a toad, turning him into a prince. Why did you decide at long last to change all that?"

"Maddie was dying and I did not know what I had until I had almost lost it. My heart was being ripped out. I had to meet her."

"But you were too late."

"Yes and no."

"What do you mean?"

Benjamin smiled and picked up Maddie from Jeni's hands and placed her on his shoulder.

"You would never understand."

"Try me."

"To believe one has to know that the strongest force in the universe is love and with it anything is conquerable."

"Even death?"

"Even death."

"I want to believe that ..."

"But you find it hard. I did too, until the day came when I learned the truth. It is a truth I saw in France, in the forties, when one man threw himself on a grenade to save his buddies. A truth evident in the eyes of a mother staring at her babe. I saw, but did not believe until..."

"Until what?"

Benjamin stroked the head of the pigeon on his shoulder. "Again, you would have to believe."

"But I do."

"Do you? To believe, you must know what it is that you believe. It is when someone else means more to you than anything else, including your own life. Do you have that depth of feeling?"

"I..."

"No. Don't answer. You will not know for sure until the time comes," Benjamin said sagely.

"Tony never mentioned you were a philosopher," Jeni said with a smile.

"I'm not really. Except when it comes to baseball. By the way, since you already conned the president and the date out of me in 'casual' conversation, let me tell you that we are presently in my apartment."

"Why would I need to know that?" Jeni said, surprised at Benjamin's perceptiveness. She had thought she was being very sly in assessing his mental status.

"No reason. How about we get out of this stuffy apartment and go for a walk in the park?"

"Sounds wonderful."

"Good. May I take your arm?"

"Why? do you need help walking?"

"No, but the sight of such a pretty lady on my arm will make all the other old geezers jealous."

"It would be my pleasure," Jeni said.

"Thank you," Benjamin smiled. Maddie, still on his shoulder, gave a questioning coo as he lifted her and put her back in the coop. Kissing her beak gently, Benjamin said "Don't worry, old girl. I will still be coming home to you. Actually, why don't we bring the kids with us. They could use the exercise."

"Why not? "Jeni agreed.

Together they climbed down the stairs, each carrying a cage filled with pigeons. They strolled and talked, each honestly enjoying the other's company. When they got to the park, Benjamin paraded Jeni past the 'old geezers' playing chess and feeding the birds, very pleased with himself.

Finding an empty bench, they sat. Benjamin opened the door and pulled out Dizzy Dean, cupped between his hands.

"Get going, D.D," he said, gentle casting him into the air. He soared into the sky, headed toward home.

Next out was Maddie. Benjamin kissed her atop her feathered head, saying "Get going, old girl." She too was hurled heavenward, but started to circle around the park.

"How come you kissed her goodbye and not Dizzy Dean?"

"She is special."

"How so?"

Looking at Maddie's flight path, he said, "Watch." Maddie finished her arch and landed atop Benjamin's shoulder.

"Amazing."

"Not really. She's jealous," the pigeon cooed sharply, as if in disagreement. "You are too. Go on, fly home," The bird refused to move. "Fine, have it your way. Are you ready to try?"

"Yes," answered Jeni.

"Have you done this before?"

"Yes. First time was on my third date with Tony." Taking out Babe, she said. "He took me and two of the birds out to dinner. Luckily, he took only me into the restaurant."

Jeni reached up and released the pigeon into the sky. Jeni stared in wonder and inhaled deeply.

"Magical, isn't it, launching them into flight like that."

"Yes."

"Almost like part of you flies up with them."

"It is the only time I almost understand his passion," Jeni confessed.

"Maddie called them angels. With them you can kiss the sky."

"Very poetic."

"Thanks, but I think it came from a sixties song. But I do write some poetry."

"Really? Tony never mentioned that."

"I never told him. I'm old school. Two men do not discuss poetry. Sissy stuff. But a man and a woman, that is another story. Maddie and I used to send each other poems. Maddie more than myself. The last poem she sent me was unfinished. She asked me to do the honors. I finally completed it and I wanted to show it to someone, other than me and the kids. Here," Benjamin said, handing Jeni a folded piece of paper. She unfolded it and read it. A tear started to trickle.

"Its...beautiful," Jeni said.

"Thank you."

"May I keep this?"

"Certainly. It is a copy. The original is upstairs."

They spent the rest of the afternoon talking. Jeni even wrote Tony a note which she tied to Dizzy Dean before sending him off.

"He will be there before you will," Benjamin said.

When evening started to fall, Benjamin walked Jeni to the bus stop and waited with her until it came.

Jeni gave Benjamin a kiss on the check and said "Thank you, I had a wonderful day."

"So did I. Best I had in a long time. Don't be a stranger. Tell Tony to let you tie on the occasional message."

"I will."

Benjamin waved until the bus drove home, then began his own trek home.

Jeni gazed thoughtfully at the poem Benjamin had given her.

> "Two old fools on borrowed wings
>   soaring through the night
> Never have our eyes met
>   yet you see though to my soul
> Past all I keep hidden
>   to the treasure within
> All that I am is nothing
>   without you to make me whole
> You have flown ahead
>   but forsake heaven's gate for my sake
> Your love keeps you behind
>   to watch over me
> Until the time we finally join
>   on our next, first and final meeting,
> When, together,
>   like angels,
> Our spirits will soar
>   beyond infinity to Evermore."

"Amazing to see such love, from someone who had never even seen her until after her death." She reverently traced the creases with her fingers, feeling the texture of the paper. A part of her flushed in shame, thinking of the shallowness of prior attractions in her life: the men and boys alike that she had liked because of looks, or material things, or the fact that they were "in" in some cliquish way. This relationship that Tony had known of was a true love between souls, with all surface masks never used. She wished that she could have met Maddie when she was alive; between Ben and Tony, she felt as if this "lady", in the purest sense of the word, would have become a precious part of her own life.

Perhaps Tony witnessing this love was what gave him such a different "feel" from the others in her past. What she had with him felt calm, and safe and sure, none of the old dating games. He said what he felt and she trusted him completely. When she thought that she was in love in the past, it was a jazzed-up high which energized her, yet ultimately drained her of herself. Being with a "catch" was a "fix" for her self-esteem, and the break-up was usually a withdrawal-like agony.

Now, she and Tony seemed as if they had been a part of each other's lives forever; with him, she was happier than she ever thought she could be.

CLAY PIGEONS

Benjamin:

I don't mean any disrespect, guy, but snap out of it! Maddie has been gone for more than a year. Nothing either you or I can do will ever change that. The way you sometimes talk and write about her, it's as if you think she is still around. You try to pass it off like you are talking about the pigeon you named after her, but sometimes I wonder. It is okay to grieve. I know your generation was taught as kids that men don't cry and to show grief is a sign of weakness. It does not have to be that way. If you miss somebody it is okay to say so, to be angry about it. It does nothing to sully who Maddie was. I know you cherish her memory. We both do and we both miss her, but life has to go on.

Say when and I'll come to Hyde Park; we'll have some drinks, do dinner. Don't close yourself off; it's not what Maddie would have wanted.

Tony

Benjamin quickly scanned the letter. Then, with a hurumph, he roughly deposited it with a number of like-minded epistles by the couch.

"Tony is beginning to get on my nerves. My generation indeed," he grumbled to his housemates. Ruby eyes blinking, the pigeons cooed a non-committal reply. Benjamin's demeanor softened, as he approached the birds' coop. He tenderly pulled out the white and gray female and perched her on his shoulder.

"Tony can be so literal; if he can't see it, it's not there." He stroked the bird's milky neck and she closed her eyes in satisfaction. "But you and I know, don't we, old girl... you and I know." The bird's silence implied consent, and he continued. "Maddie is as alive to me as she ever was ... why should I have to leave these four walls to venture into a bright and barren world outside? I have you and the rest of my flock. Still, I guess I have to humor the boy."

Tony,

Thank you for your concern, but it is misplaced. I am fine and am content in my old age. I do go out everyday for my walk; sometimes for a change I even head up your way to the Commons. Yes, I have enough of my facilities to negotiate public transportation. My generation even gets a discount. I walk around the park and watch the families feeding the squirrels and pigeons. Then, sitting on a bench eating a hot dog and pretzel, I try to imagine what madness possesses joggers as they race by, in a hurry to get back to where they started. Sometimes I even wander over to Quincy Market and take in a street performer show. What the heck, they are free. I only wish they would vary their material a bit. Some of them get old the third or forth time. My favorite is the drummer who plays on parts of his kitchen. I tried to make music that way once. Actually I just kept dropping a bunch of pots and pans. No music ensued. Just lots of noise and a big mess.

Next time I'm up that way I will stop by and take you up on that drink.

Please stop pestering me about my habits - you are worse than John! Not that I didn't enjoy your lady friend Jeni's company. I am far from adverse to spending a day with a beautiful young woman, but your motives were too oblivious. Really, sending a nurse to check up on me! She acted like more of a psychology major than a nurse. She did learn a thing or two about the angels, I dare say.

Did I pass the sanity test? I would have stayed up and studied the night before had I known, but I was seeing my doctor the next day and had to cram for my urine test.

On a personal note, Jeni is a gem. If you let her go, you are the crazy one.

Be well.

Benjamin

P.S.- Please give Jeni the enclosed note. Thanks.

"Stubborn old goat - head's as hard as the tin cans he probably chews," Tony grumbled upon reading Benjamin's reply. "I shouldn't worry so much about him, but Maddie wanted me to keep an eye on him."

He called to Jeni, who was precariously balanced over

the bathroom sink, attempting to draw a straight line under her eye. "Jeni, Ben got your number good. I thought I told you not to be obvious about checking him out."

Silently cursing her lack of steady aim, she wiped her eyelid with her finger and tried again. "I was, Tony; that man was just too antagonistic. You would have thought that I was grilling him at some murder trial, the way he reacted to my casual questions."

"That's Benjamin," Tony replied with resignation. "Well, at least he agreed to a drink together. He was impressed by you, though. Sent you a note."

"He did? How sweet," Jeni said as she opened it and read it.

> Jeni,
> Thank you for taking the time to spend with an old man. You brightened my day. Feel free to visit anytime.
> If Tony ever gives you any grief, tell me and I will set him straight. He is a very lucky man.
> Be well.
>
> Sincerely,
> Benjamin

Jeni penned a quick note and handed it to Tony. "Send this to him when you reply. Benjamin has some odd habits, but he is not a danger to himself or anyone else, so you don't have to worry about him. Pretty smart old guy. A romantic."

"Benjamin?" Tony stared at her in amazement.

"Yes. I read this poem he wrote for Maddie. Apparently, she started it and he finished it."

"Not bad." Tony announced as he scanned it.

"Not bad? It is beautiful. No wonder Benjamin said men don't share poetry with other men. It's just not appreciated," Jeni said.

Finishing up his own morning routine, Tony gathered up his keys and wallet and entered the bathroom. Giving Jeni a light kiss on her neck, he smiled at her reflection. "See you tonight?"

She shook her head. "Afraid not - remember? Spring break starts this weekend and I've got to get packed. When I get back, no more classes. It is straight on to clinicals. I can't wait to get started working in a hospital."

Returning his grimace her reminder caused, she continued. "Besides, I want to check on my Uncle Tyler. No one at home is talking to me about it, but he's been sick for the past six or seven months and his symptoms sound an awful lot like your friend Maddie's. Frankly, Tony, I'm scared."

Turning to him, she lightly touched his cheek; he covered her hand with his own and pressed it tightly against his face. Nodding wordlessly, he gathered her up and they shared a moment of mutual comfort.

"I know," Tony confessed. "Every time I see Ben, I search for signs that its starting with him. But he seems healthy; its just his mental state I worry about. He seems obsessed about Maddie - it started when he named that pigeon he got after Maddie died."

"He does kiss that bird."

"You are kidding me?"

"Nope. But she is special. Flies then lands on his shoulder. Seems almost to understand conversation," Jeni said as Zeus walked into the bathroom and started drinking out of the toilet. "Just like some dogs I know, right, Zeus?"

At the mention of his name, Zeus walked over to try to lick Jeni's face as she scratched behind his ears with both hands.

"I wish that he would get an additional hobby besides just the pigeons," Tony said.

"You can't change someone who does not want to be changed."

"I know."

They stood, each lost in their own thoughts, until Tony mentally shook himself and stepped back. Jeni busily ended her primping and they walked together to the door. She softly said, "I'll see you in a couple of weeks. Try not to worry so much about Benjamin. If there's one thing I determined about him, its that he's a real fighter. He did however give me an idea. He told me he would take the birds with him down to New York and let them fly back from Yankee Stadium. The Bronx is not far from Queens. Could I take Wings with me and send him back with a message when I get home?"

Tony thought a minute. "Take Raphael instead. He once made the trip from Long Island, which is about the same distance."

"Thanks. How fast do pigeons fly?"

"About forty five miles per hour."

"Wow, so the trip will take about five hours?"

"Less. Raphael doesn't have to follow the roads," Tony said, packing up Raphael in a carrying cage and giving Jeni paper and a leg carrier.

"See you in two weeks," Jeni said, as she and Tony kissed and hugged passionately.

After their good-byes, Tony replied, "Take care, Jeni. have a safe trip. Even though you are sending Raph, call me when you get to your folk's home so I know that you made it safely. Bye, Zeus," Tony said, giving the golden retriever a big hug. "The railroad people are going to think you are a zookeeper, bringing all these animals with you."

"Poor Zeus, he hates the cage."

"He would hate being without you for two weeks even

more. I'll be leaving for school as soon as I pen a quick note for Ben."

Just a few more weeks for you too."

"Amen."

Tony walked Jeni out and watched as she and the dog walked out of sight. He ran back inside, looked at his watch and decided to send the note later.

Subject: Welcome to NY
From: Esquire
To: Nightingale

Jeni,

Welcome to the wonderful world of e-mail. Never had time to use this before, but unfortunately phone bills run into bucks, which neither of us have much of at this point. Next year at this time we will both be working and that won't be a problem. Regardless, I will call you tonight.

Raphael got back safely with your message. Thanks. Glad the train ride was good.

I miss you already. (Pathetic, aren't I?)

Talk to you later :)

Love,
Tony

Subject: Lonely in NY
From: Nightingale
To: Esquire

Tony,

Not bad. Did not know if you could write a note that was not attached to a pigeon's leg. :-)~
(< raspberries...hah!)

I enjoyed our talk earlier. (What do you mean you will call me? I called you, you goofball.) I miss you, too :(And you are not pathetic. I think you are adorable, but what do I know?

Like I told you on the phone, something weird is going on with my Uncle Tyler and nobody will tell me. I called him twice, but got a message that his phone had been disconnected. My mother promised they would come clean with me in the morning. Of course now I can't sleep so I went online with my Dad's computer. I tried counting sheep first but it did not work. Now I am counting you. You look quite cute jumping over the fence in wool underwear.

I will talk to you tomorrow.

(: XOXO :)

Love, Jeni

The phone rang early the next morning. Tony picked up the phone cheerfully and immediately heard the sorrow in Jeni's voice and it ripped at his heart. He asked with concern, "Jeni, Hon, what's wrong?"

"This morning I told Mom that I wanted to visit Uncle Tyler. She finally came clean with me. She told me that he no longer lived in his house, that he had been "transferred" to one of those bubble sanitariums in New York City - Tony, I was right, he has TADS. He has become an Innuendo." The tearful tone of her voice gave way to actual sobbing.

"He left over three weeks ago; no one told me why they would not tell me. They just kept saying it was for my own good, as if I could not decide for myself. He's my favorite uncle; they had no right not to tell me. I didn't get to hug him goodbye. Now even if I go visit him, we can never touch again."

Tony felt almost numbed by the news. "Jeni, I'm so sorry. Will he be OK ?"

"I don't know. He should be, I guess. I am going to see him now. I just needed to talk."

"Anytime. Is there anything I can do?"

"Just being there helps. Just promise me you will never hide something from me for 'my own good'."

"I promise."

"I gotta run. I will talk to you later."

Jeni had never been one to hate hospitals but this was different. This one she hated. No matter what people say, hospitals are places of hope and healing. Sometimes hope remains forever unrealized, but it is still there.

Here in this bubble that crucial element was lacking. Care amounted to a life sentence, death the only reprieve. That was what her Uncle Tyler had been condemned to; that was what Jeni hated.

He had always loved the outdoors. Uncle Tyler had

taught her to fly her first kite and took her and Bobby, her brother camping every year since they could first toddle. He had been the one that had given her Zeus back when he was a puppy to help her with her homesickness. He was the goofy, crazy uncle that the rest of the family was embarrassed by because he did what he wanted without regard for who was watching. What he usually wanted was to make Jeni laugh and he succeeded without fail.

Now Jeni sat and waited in a room that reminded her of a prison visiting room. Two seats separated by Plexiglas, a phone on either side to convey words across the barrier. An eternity later, he walked in.

Jeni had feared he would be so sick she would not recognize him. Uncle Tyler had lost about ten pounds, but was unmistakable from his balding head to his bushy goatee. He was dressed in plain blue surgeon scrubs. Upon seeing her, he ran forward in slow motion, arms outstretched in mock imitation of a man running across a field to greet his long lost love. He dashed right up the chair onto the counter, crashing right into the window. With a flourish, he crumpled to the floor.

"Uncle Tyler!" Jeni jumped to her feet and shouted. "Are you okay?" Her voice did not carry through the barrier, so when Tyler stumbled to his knees and lifted up his phone she did the same.

Tyler crossed his eyes and stuck his tongue out of the side of his mouth. "Mommy, is that you?"

"Unc, cut it out! You frightened me," Jeni said, smiling despite herself. She thought *every damn time I see him he makes me laugh, even now.*

"Sorry. Got a little excited seeing my favorite niece and all."

"Unc, I am your only niece."

"Well, at least you know I'm not lying. Now how about a kiss for your favorite uncle?"

"How?" Jeni asked, throwing up her arms in exasperation.

"Put your cheek up against the glass," Tyler said. Jeni did and Tyler gave the glass in front of her a quick peck. Jeni chuckled and shook her head.

"My turn," she said into the phone. Tyler obliged by pressing the entire side of his face against the glass, becoming a caricature of himself. Jeni returned the kiss and they both sat back down.

"How are you, my dear?" Tyler asked.

"Good, until I heard about you. They did not tell me until this morning or I would have come down from school sooner."

"I know," Tyler smiled. "That is why they did not tell you."

"You let them get away with that?"

"It was your last semester and finals week. They made sense."

"But I did not get a chance to say goodbye."

"I'm not dead, you know."

"I'm sorry. I know you are not. As an almost nurse I should know better than to talk to you like that. How bad is it?"

"Mid-stage two. I had to get in immediately or...."

"I understand."

"Did they tell you the rest?"

"What rest?"

"I'm in here temporarily only. I'm signed up to be transferred to a bubble village."

"Village?"

"These bubble villages are popping up all over. Apparently TADS is profitable. "

"Where is it?"

"Called Cheshire House. It's down in Richmond."

"Virginia?"

"Yep."

"But that is so far away."

"I know, but I had to get in. It is not open yet but to guarantee a spot I had to give them some cash up front."

"How much?"

"A lot. More than I had. Your folks chipped in. But that means they do not have enough to pay the rent on your apartment in Boston."

Jeni's heart dropped through the floor.

"What?"

"I am sorry. I know how much you like it up there and how much you care for Tony. How is my paesano doing? Things between you two still good?"

"Things are wonderful. He is definitely the one."

"Hold on to him with both hands. When you find the one it makes all the difference. I still miss your Aunt Sally and it has been five years. If only we had kids, but at least we did have nieces and nephews: all the fun with a fraction of the responsibility. But I am sorry to come between you and Tony."

"You are not coming between us. So I won't be able to go back up to Boston right away. My classes are done - all A's and a B," Jeni said. Tyler nodded proudly. "Only thing left is my hospital work. I can do that down here in the city. I will just have to live in Woodside while I do it. A little distance won't come between us. As soon as I finish, I can get a job and move back up there."

Jeni meant every word she said, but she was still hurt and downhearted. It was not that she could not be without Tony; she did not want to be without him. Two days had been rough but three to six months? She filed that away to worry about later. Tyler was her first concern right now. "Besides, you helped pay for my tuition. If it was not for you, I would not have been able to go away in the first place. This is my chance to pay you back."

"That money was a gift. No need for payback, but thanks anyway. I tell you lately I love you?"

"Nope," Jeni said.

"Well, I love you."

"I love you too, Unc."

A voice came over the phone line. "Your visit has four minutes remaining."

"What was that?" Jeni asked.

"Visiting space is limited, so we only have thirty minutes."

"That stinks."

"If you think that stinks, you should smell the recycled air in here. How is Zeus?"

"Clueless as ever."

"Send him my best. Scratch him behind the ears for me. Tony too."

"Sure but how do you know Tony likes his ears scratched? Something you two have been keeping from me?"

"No. Nothing. I don't even know about his birthmark."

"He does not have a birthmark."

"Worth a shot."

The voice interrupted again. "Two minutes remaining. Please complete your visit at this time. Thank you."

"Guess we better say goodbye," Tyler said, his jovial mood sobering.

"Are they treating you well in there?" Jeni asked.

"As well as can be expected. The living conditions kind of remind me of Korea except I don't have to shoot at anybody and the uniforms are blue," Tyler said, referring to his scrubs.

"I wish I could hug you, Uncle Tyler," Jeni said.

"I do too, sweetheart, but it's out of our hands."

"If there is anything I can do for you let me know."

"Visit."

"I will. Anything else?"

"I will let you know," Tyler said, face deadpan and jokes forgotten for the moment. "Be good." Tyler stood and turned away from his niece, trying to hide his face but she saw the tear escape each eye.

Before he could walk away, she started to bang on the glass. An orderly standing watch gave her a dirty look. Tyler turned and picked up the phone Jeni was pointing to.

Before either of them could speak the voice interrupted again. "Your time has expired. Please exit the visiting area as others are waiting."

"What is it dear? My time is up," Tyler said, wiping away hidden tears.

"So? Since when do you listen to rules?" Jeni countered.

Tyler smiled. "True. What can I do for you?"

"Don't I get a kiss goodbye?" Jeni asked.

"Of course," Tyler answered. This time Jeni squished her face up against the glass, like some squashed bug on a windshield. Tyler kissed her distorted cheek. Their positions reversed and she smooched his cheek back. Tyler pointed for her to pick up the phone. The voice continued to drone on about their time being up.

"I have too much time on my hands in here so I have been learning pantomime. Watch. Man under glass." Tyler said as he stood on the counter and pressed his palms against the glass in imitation of a mine.

Jeni covered her face, giggling. An orderly in an environmental suit grabbed Tyler's arm and pulled him down and across the room toward the exit. Tyler exaggerated like he was being pulled forcibly, throwing his body forward and his legs back. He blew her a kiss, which she caught and returned one of her own.

"Every damn time," Jeni said, laughing and shaking her head happily.

She laughed so much she forgot to cry until Tyler was gone.

The walls shook and the rafters rocked with the wrath of a daughter spurned.

"How could you keep all this from me!?" Jeni demanded of her parents. Her father sat quiet and calm while her mother matched Jeni's ranting with her own.

"Kitten..." her father started.

"Don't call me kitten, right now. You both lied to me," Jeni said.

"What do you mean we lied?" her mother shouted. "We did no such thing."

"You did not tell me about Uncle Tyler until it was too late for me to say goodbye in person. Sin of omission."

"You would have missed your finals," her mother said.

"Maybe, but I could have gotten a hardship extension because of a family emergency. And you still have not told me the next bit of news that will shake up my life. Unc had to tell me."

"You mean about staying in Boston," her father said.

"That is exactly what I mean."

"We did not want to upset you," her father said.

"A little too late for that, don't you think?"

"Tyler had to go Innuendo. There was no other choice," her mother said.

"Of course he had to go Innuendo. He has TADS. I understand that. I just don't understand or accept why you did not tell me."

"We were trying to protect you," her mother said.

"From what? Life? The truth? You can't protect me from either. I am a woman, not a little girl. You have to start treating me like one."

"What difference would it have made?" said her mother.

"Plenty. I still would have been mad and upset but at fate, not the two of you. I could have seen Unc one last time face to face. I could have had my stuff packed up to move down here. I would have had time to prepare mentally. I could have given Tony time to prepare."

"He is not the only boy in the world, you know. You might meet someone here in Queens," offered her mother.

"Tony is the only man for me."

"You are young yet," said her mother

"I am twenty three, Mom. By the time you were my age you had three kids."

"Oh my god! Are you pregnant?" her mother asked, shocked.

"No," Jeni said curtly. "Why do you always assume the worst? Why do you treat me like a child?"

"If you don't like the way I do things, why don't you just go back to Boston?" her mother asked.

"Maybe I will," Jeni replied.

"Where would you live?" asked her mother, on the defensive.

"I will just move in with Tony," Jeni said with a smile, knowing with that line it was point and game.

"You would not. You could not," her mother stammered.

"I will be in my room," Jeni informed, turning to leave.

"Jeni, come back here," her father said. Reluctantly, Jeni did. "Stop this, both of you. Jeni, we did what we thought was best. With hindsight, it's clear that we were wrong. We are very sorry. Aren't we, Mother?"

"Yes," her mother said softly but honestly. "But she said..."

"That she would move in with Tony," answered her father. "But only because you had backed her into a corner. Despite what was said, I know my little girl... sorry... my grown woman. Jeni is a good Catholic and she would never live with a man she was not married to. I know we raised a daughter who will do the right thing. Am I right, Jeni?"

"Yes," Jeni safely said.

"And I know that as soon as you get your nursing license you will be moving back to Boston. You will just have to give your mother some time to get used to the idea. She was hoping you would move back to Queens. Now the two of you make up because I do not want my daughter's last months living in our home to be spent in battle."

Jeni and her mother looked at each other awkwardly.

"I'm sorry," Jeni said.

"Me too," replied her mother. "With everything going on with Tyler I have been on edge. I shouldn't have taken it out on you. I know you will miss Tony. Money will be tight but we can help you with the occasional train ticket. Tony is welcome to visit here anytime."

Mother and daughter embraced. "Thanks, Mom. You really don't mind him staying in my room?" Jeni said. Her mother pulled back, eyes wide and mouth agape. Jeni grinned. "Just kidding, Mom. Now why don't you help me try to find a local hospital to do my clinicals at?"

Only a week later than he intended, Tony walked to his desk and wrote:

Benjamin:
Ouch! You wound me - such lack of trust! We'll talk about your paranoia this Saturday at ten, at Little George's Bar. If you have any problems with date or time, send me a note.

Tony

P.S. - Jeni sent you a note too. Trust me, I know how lucky I am to have found her.

Moving to his balcony and to a small pigeon coop, Tony pulled out Babe, relaxing next to Michael and Wings. After properly greeting all three of the bright-eyed beauties, he placed the note around Babe's leg and sent him aloft. Tony then turned on the computer to check for E-mail from Jeni.

Jeni had managed to find a clinical in Queens, but there where two catches. One, she had to start immediately, but that meant she would finish early, and two, she had to work the eleven to seven am shift. With Tony working part time in a legal aide office until ten at night, it did not leave them much chance to talk on the phone. E-mail had become their primary source of communication.

He had two messages, both from Jeni:

Subject: Clinicals
To: Esquire
From: Nightingale

Tony,
Work at the hospital has been good. I have been working in the ICU. (Intensive care unit, for you lawyer types.) Have been seeing too many trauma patients. One guy, only twenty two years old, was in a motor cycle wreck. They say he may be permanently brain damaged. Promise me you will never ride a motorcycle or at least never without a helmet.

A pair of firsts. I did my first IV line. I found the vein on the second try. I also inserted my first catheter. Stop crossing your legs. It was on a woman, but tomorrow I get to try it on a man. :-(~

The late shift stinks, but because it is so quiet they are letting me do much more than the nursing students on day shifts.

I have been to see Uncle Tyler twice. He says "hi" to his "paesano". Zeus sends a lick and his wet nose on your back. Mother and I have not argued in three days... a new record.

I have Saturday off. I will call you then. Right now I need sleep desperately. With luck, I will dream of you.

Love, Jeni

Tony smiled and called up the second note.

Subject: Oatmeal Alert
To: Esquire
From: Nightingale

Tony,

I miss you. I really do, more than I thought I could. This is horrible. I thought I could handle it, (:Keep your mind out of the gutter, please. :) and I can. I just don't like it. I hope you know how much I love you. I woke up hugging Zeus and thinking of you. I love the furball, but he is no substitute for you.

I should be able to come up in three weekends. I can't wait.

Give yourself a hug for me.
XOXOXOXOXOXOXO.

Love, Jeni

Tony read and felt a warmth flow over him. He missed her every bit as much as she did him. The realization that he wanted to spend the rest of his life with her washed over him. Evermore, as Benjamin's poem put it. With the realization came a plan.

THE GREAT PIGEON HUNT

Babe was waiting at Benjamin's fire escape window when Benjamin returned from grocery shopping. After letting the bird in and removing and reading the letter, he put his groceries away. Babe was welcomed by all his fellow pigeons in the coop, including Maddie, who was resting on top of the cage.

As soon as the food was up and all greetings given, Benjamin began preparing dinner. Seeds were generously dished out for his angel family and a TV dinner was quickly warmed up for himself. A separate bowl of seed was poured for Maddie. She joined him at the coffee table, eyeing her dinner as Ben perched himself on the couch's arm. After plunking both of their dinners on the table, he rose and turned on the TV. Maddie observed his move with a look of disdain.

"Don't give me that look, Maddie. I am not too cheap to buy a color TV - I just don't believe in throwing useful things away; its wasteful. This one may be over 20 years old, but it still works great. Besides, if you had come back as a schnauzer you would not be able to tell the difference. It's not my fault birds see in color."

Maddie cooed in reluctant agreement. As she pecked at her seed, Benjamin returned to the couch with note in hand.

"Got a letter from Tony. He wants me to meet him for drinks, even set a time for the day after tomorrow. Saturday." Maddie looked up from her bowl of seed and cooed again. "Yes, I should go, I guess. I will send my RSVP tomorrow."

Seemingly satisfied by his answer, she noisily fluttered and returned to her meal.

"I also got a note from Jeni," Benjamin said, peaking Maddie's interest. "Says she enjoyed our visit. I still got it," Maddie threw her head back and cooed. "She said she enjoyed meeting all the kids; especially you, Maddie. The girl knows quality when she sees it," Benjamin said.

Maddie cooed agreement. "Now be quiet for awhile. The 5:00 news is coming on. They said there was something on about TADS."

"These stories just ahead. Anti war protesters arrested in a march outside the White House denouncing the U.S. police action in Central America. Surrogate mother sues corporation to keep a most unusual child. Wombers and supporters lobby Congress for Womber Clone Rights and an end to body tattooing."

"But first, our top story. The Federal Bureau of Disease Control today released a report stating that they believe they have determined the method of transmission and spread of the TADS virus."

"TADS was first diagnosed four years ago in the United States and has quickly reached epidemic proportions in the last two years, spanning forty-two states and sixteen countries."

"That was before when you were diagnosed," Benjamin turned to his feathered companion.

The new reporter continued on. "Like the AIDS pandemic and unlike the recent staph A virus scares, a cure for the illness itself has still not been found. Various possibilities of a source have been purposed. Water sources, casual body contact, sexually transmitted diseases... all have been explored as possible sources, with negative results. Many of our listeners may even remember the allegations that surfaced last month stating that the TADS virus was developed in the United States as a form of viral warfare. With such uncertainty, there is no wonder rumors abound.

The virus appears to be most widespread in urban areas, less so in rural parts of the country, cutting across all cultural barriers with no apparent rhyme or reason.

After extensive research plotting outbreak areas and correlating similarities in victims' lifestyles, habits, and other data, the Center revealed that they believe that the virus is carried in the fecal droppings of urban-found birds, particularly pigeons. A presidential commission is being formed to work closely with the FBDC to explore containment options to minimize further spread of the disease. Due to the extreme mobility of the carrier pigeons, it is possible that drastic methods such as extermination squads for the birds may be considered.

In other news......"

Shock momentarily froze Benjamin's reaction to the grizzly news. He sat, slack-jawed, staring first at the TV set and then at Maddie and the rest of his flock.

"That can't be what I heard. Birds can't be causing this plague, not the angels." He crouched in front of the TV and frantically turned from station to station, searching for more information. Not finding any, he returned to the couch, to wait for the six o'clock report.

Within minutes, he restlessly rose, appetite gone. He numbly deposited the remains of his supper in the trash. As he stood at the sink with the water drumming hollowly on his plate, Maddie landed on his shoulder, in an attempt to comfort him.

To Benjamin and the bird's surprise, when Maddie brushed his shoulder, he recoiled from her touch. His fearful reflex almost knocked her to the floor; only a quick maneuver prevented such a catastrophe. Landing on the counter, she puffed up and clacked her beak with fright and indignation.

"Maddie! Are you all right?" Benjamin gasped, not

believing his own reaction. "I don't know what came over me; truly, I would never hurt you." He moved toward the bird, but Maddie fluttered back to the couch and eyed him warily.

Benjamin returned to his seat and sank his head into his hands, moaning. "I was remembering the funeral... and how the TADS must have been contracted..." He glanced toward his pigeon coops and for a moment was lulled by their soft cooing. With despair in his voice, he wondered, "Which one of you brought such a dark thing into my life? Why did I not catch it also?"

He turned to Maddie. "But not you, Maddie, never you!" The opening credits for the six o'clock news caught his attention. "Let me listen again; maybe I just misunderstood what was said."

He did not. The later program detailed precautions that needed to be taken to avoid contamination: avoid parks and other areas where pigeons tend to group; don't hang out laundry where it can be soiled; thoroughly wash face and hands every time you return from going outside and so on. Animal rights activists spoke out against knee-jerk killing reactions to the announcement, quoting a government report estimating roughly twenty percent of the pigeon population to be possible carriers.

The activists also argued that mass destruction of urban birdlife could upset the ecosystem and so caution must be taken in dealing with the problem. Other groups were not so charitable, demanding government action: immediate, swift, and deadly.

Benjamin listened to all the divergent voices, finally handing down his own judgment to the talk about killing. "Madness! By morning, wiser heads will have taken action - I hope."

He may have hoped, but even he did not believe his own words, knowing human nature as he did. He feared that what he witnessed on the TV was just the tip of the iceberg. Benjamin went to sleep praying for the first time since Maddie's funeral.

Friday dragged slowly by. Benjamin stayed in, but he did send Dizzy Dean out with a message for Tony. A wave of concern crossed Ben's mind as he watched his fan-tailed friend take to the sky; he tried to brush it from his mind.

Fortunately, the winged messenger made it to his destination without mishap. Pulling the note from Dizzy Dean's leg, Tony placed the bird in his coop with the others, then went inside.

He read:

Tony:
  I will meet you at Little George's, Saturday - ten o'clock is fine. Will need to talk to you about all this hysteria. We may have to hide our angels or the mobs may get them.

            Benjamin

P.S.- This can't be true, can it? The birds would never have hurt Maddie; they would never hurt anyone. Besides, we would both be sick ourselves, wouldn't we? I feel fine. How about you?

Not for the first time, Tony wondered, perhaps even imagined, that he had some of the symptoms. He worried, "I should get rid of the pigeons, but how? To let them loose into the skies would be signing their death warrants. No pound nor animal shelter wanted birds, let alone pigeons." Then there was the hardest part: explaining it to Benjamin. Ben would view it as moral cowardice - perhaps it was. Regardless, Tony put his safety first.

It was simple. Surely Ben would see that. Tony penned a quick note:

> *Benjamin:*
>   *See you tomorrow.*
>
>   *Tony*

It was tied to Dizzy Dean's leg and D.D. was sent off into Boston's smog filled skies.

Saturday morning came soon enough. It was a short walk for Benjamin to the bus stop which took him to the Forest Hills subway station onto the Orange line. A quick transfer let him off beneath the Boston Commons. His nerves were frazzled, and, as it was only 9:20, he thought that he had plenty of time for a relaxing stroll on the footpaths until he met with Tony.

The Commons was mobbed, especially for a Saturday. No one else seemed to be there for relaxation. It looked more like a war zone to Benjamin, who felt as if he was having a flash back to occupied France in World War II.

Literally dozens, maybe even hundreds, of people were armed with weapons varying from sling shots to shotguns. The police did nothing for the moment, out manned and out gunned. They stood by watching about twenty people;

men, women, and children, standing in a circle, throwing bread crumbs on the ground, laying a diabolical trap. They stood perfectly still while scores of pigeons were pecking at the bait; when enough pigeons were encircled, a large net was dropped. All the birds, save those few whose reflexes were a mite swifter than their fellows, were hopelessly snared. Half of the urban trappers stepped on the edge of the netting; the other half, wearing rubber gloves and homemade face masks, advanced on the hapless avians. With clubs and bats they proceeded to bludgeon the small creatures to death.

Many were grinning with sadistic glee. A father, as calm as if they were at bat Day at Fenway Park, corrected his six year old son's swing, instructing him to aim for the heads.

Within moments, the netted carnage was over; a slew of bloody-feathered corpses littered the lawn. Several other nearby sites showed the tactics had worked at least four times before.

Others were shooting the birds with BB guns, rifles... one person was even using a bow and arrow. Some high school age toughs had sandwiched in between them a wounded bird. They chased after it with their handguns in an attempt to catch the pigeon in their crossfire. Sensing the danger, the pigeon tried to take to the air. However, only three feet off the ground, her wings betrayed her and she fell. In falling, the bird dropped below the line of bullets the youths had already fired. One boy was not as lucky as the bird, for his friend's bullet caught him right in the heart.

"Jimmy!" his friend cried out, running to his side. It was too late for Jimmy, but not too late for the tears; they flowed both for Jimmy by his friends and for the slaughtered birds by a grief-shattered Benjamin. Too late...the police, now that riot team reinforcements arrived, now that a human was hurt, moved in to try to control the crowds.

Benjamin stumbled from the park, physically ill from what he had witnessed. Crossing Beacon Street, passing by the State House, he leaned against a brick building as he tried to regain his strength.

In the alleyway behind him, Benjamin heard a soft, dragging sound. Peering into the alley, he saw a huge rat with a dead pigeon in his overstretched jaws; he was trying to pull it behind a pile of trash. Benjamin moaned at the horror, for the bird looked sickeningly like his Dizzy Dean. When the rodent discovered that he was being watched, he hissed through clenched teeth and attempted to pull faster. The bird's head bounced roughly against the black asphalt as the rat dragged it away; with this final scene, Benjamin's gorge rose and he proceeded to throw up.

Finally reaching the bar, he found Tony waiting there already. Climbing on the empty stool beside him, Benjamin grunted to the bartender, "Whiskey...double...straight," before shakily turning to greet his friend. "Oh, Tony," he sadly said.

"Hey, Benjamin; what's with the hard stuff? I thought beer was your drink."

"Not today. The insanity outside has left a foul taste in my mouth. Tony, angels are falling from the sky for the second time since Time began... men are killing them in the streets."

Tony stared into the bar mirror, reading the disbelief on his friend's face and noting the guilt covering his own. Quickly dropping his eyes, Tony related his own horror stories.

"I know how awful it is, Benjamin. I was at the waterfront along Storrow Drive this morning and it was as

if everyone there had gone mad. People were throwing
rocks, bottles, you name it, at the pigeons. Kids were
climbing trees and shaking the limbs to get the birds to fly
so they could get a better shot at them. Of course, that
made things worse, because all the pigeon poop which
was stuck in the trees came raining down on everyone.
People were screaming, and several women actually
jumped into the river in their panic to get the stuff off."

Tony's last description did at least get a chuckle from
Benjamin, as he imagined the women's plunge. Ben wryly
noted, "Knowing the condition of that water, I would say
that they would have been safer with the crap on."

Tony gravely continued, "There's a homeless guy that
hangs around Storrow Drive - he's got some kind of
thyroid problem that makes his eyes bug out, so people
call him Peepers. He was down there throwing out poisoned birdseed. Said that he was going to kill the birds
before they killed him. Peepers was even selling bags of
the seed to people."

Silently, he recalled Peeper's words. The wiry little
man sat cross legged on the grass, with little bags of seed
piled to one side of him and a crude "POISON BIRD-
SEED - $1" sign on the other side. "Them birds kept me
fed fer de past four years, with me catchin' them and
cookin' them. Now, I can't eat them!"

His Adam's apple bobbled as he choked back tears. "I
gots ta eat, ya know? Figures I can get some money fer
food if I sell some of this seed. Upside is, for the last few
days I makes about $20 a piece cleanin' pigeon poop from
car windows. I used to only get a buck if I was lucky. Now
that I found out it could kill me, I don't do it no more.
Tried to have the cops charge the ones who had me do it
before I knew with attempted murder, but the cops told me
to get lost. I made about two hundred the last two days,
but that don't go far. Found some rat's poison in de
dumpster and mixed it with a bag o' birdseed ol' lady

McCaffrey gave me to bait de birds."

As Tony sat quietly on the bar stool, remembering, he felt the weight in his coat pocket and cupped his hand around it. He traced the outline of two small bags of birdseed resting there; he then slipped his hand away, hoping that Ben had not noticed. A hot flush of shame raced across his face and he began to cough to cover the change.

"What's the matter, youngster?" Benjamin asked. "Drink too strong for you?"

"No," Tony whispered softly, staring down into his beer. However, not one to hide behind his own cowardice, Tony bit the bullet and decided to confess his fears. "Benjamin, I hate to mention this; you may hate me for it, but it needs to be said. At least one of the birds is probably a carrier for the TADS virus. Maddie's dying from it is proof of that. There is no way to tell which bird it is. We may both be in danger."

"You are talking nonsense; wouldn't we have gotten it by now?"

"Maybe, maybe not. All I know is that there is no cure. People are scared, have been for years; only now they have something to lash out at. People may attack us for having pigeons."

"I hope not. Its horrible out there as it is now. I saw a rat dragging off a pigeon carcass that looked a lot like Dizzy Dean. I'm glad that he is still with you."

Tony shook his head. "No, he's not, Benjamin. I sent him back to you yesterday. He never got there?"

Benjamin's face grew white. "No... my God! He's still out there!"

"Or..." Both were silent with the possibilities. Then Tony said, "Bartender, another round for my friend and me." When the drinks came, both men raised their glasses.

"To Dizzy Dean," they toasted their fallen angel.

Returning to the predicament at hand, Tony said, "I was going to suggest that we set them free to protect ourselves before all this happened." Noting Benjamin's firm mouth and angry eyes, he continued, "It wouldn't work, even without people trying to kill them. One: they were all raised in captivity and I doubt they would fare well totally on their own. Two: it wouldn't keep them away from us, because they would continue to come home to roost." Looking hopefully at Ben, he suggested, "Could we have them tested to at least see which one it was?"

Benjamin sadly replied, "Too new and expensive a test, Tony; vets would not have anything available yet. However, we should probably get tested."

Tony nodded agreement. "Then that leaves us with only one option," Tony said, first fingering, then pulling the two bags of poisoned seed out of his pocket and placing them on the bar.

"And what is that?" Benjamin eyed the bags warily, already knowing the answer.

Tony silently handed him a bag.

"No! Never, it's wrong!" Benjamin practically screamed as he hurled the bag to the floor. Other patrons in the bar turned to stare curiously at the two men, then returned to their own food and drink.

Keeping his voice low, Tony caught Benjamin's gaze and held it. "Maybe... but you can't tell me you haven't thought about it."

"No, I can't," Benjamin fell quiet in his shame. "But I rejected it. They are my friends, my family; they're as important to me as any favored pet. I am not cruel enough, not strong enough to kill them." He looked pleadingly at Tony. "They have souls too. They deserve to live every bit as much as I do."

"I understand. I really do. But tell me, Benjamin: in a choice between their lives or yours - who would you pick?"

"I pray that it does not come to that."

"It already has," Tony said, picking up the poison seed from the floor and again handing it to Benjamin. "Here, take it. You don't have to use it. Just keep your options open."

Benjamin looked at the tiny sack in his hand. Weighed down by fear and guilt, it seemed much too heavy for its size. His first instinct was to again throw it down, but he did not. Instead he said simply and with great sadness, "Okay." Pocketing the bag, he finished the rest of his shot in a single gulp.

Benjamin fought between the impulse to delay the return to his apartment and the desire to bolt through the battleground he was witnessing. With every step, the small bag tugged at him, slowing his step, while quickening his heartbeat. "What to do, what to do?" drummed in his head in time to his footsteps.

Upon arriving at his apartment house, he noticed several tenants in a group by the entrance. Their conversation abruptly ceased when Benjamin began to move toward them. One of the more belligerent neighbors, Mike, loudly remarked to no one in particular, "You know, he owns pigeons." The tone in his voice went straight up Benjamin's spine. Matching the man's anger, Benjamin fixed his glare on his neighbor's face until he took a step backwards from the older man. His bluff called, Mike dropped his eyes but raised his voice. "Yeah, right up above our apartments... they fly in and out of his window. He's gonna kill us with them birds. I tell you..."

Ben did not hear the rest of the ranting as he slammed the heavy outer door shut between himself and the embryonic mob. Lightheaded and trembling, he walked up the stairs to his apartment.

Once inside his loft, Benjamin splashed cold water on his face and neck, gulping air and fighting for composure. He leaned his forehead on the wall beside the sink for an eternity, silently mouthing an incoherent prayer into the void. Fear's bile burnt his throat and he wondered for the thousandth time since Maddie died if he had overstayed his time on this earth.

Time did not quickly settle the cauldron of insanity. The news dryly reported case after case of slaughter: nettings, clubbings, shootings, gassings... the city sanitation department crews began to refuse to touch the rotting carcasses littering the streets and the odor became overwhelming. There were scenes of rats, multiplied due to the increased food supply, gorging on the putrid remains.

Benjamin shut off the TV, swearing that it would stay off for the duration; he could stand it no longer. With tears in his eyes, he finally told his flock about Dizzy Dean. Maddie flew to his shoulder, trying to nuzzle his ear with her beak.

"Thanks, old girl, but not even you can make me feel better this time." He returned the nuzzle by stroking her back with his finger. Murmuring in an ominous tone, he said, "I don't know what to do; the lot of you may be killers." In an even more conspiring whisper, he added, "One of them may have caused your death, Maddie; it's true. Tony is terrified, poor kid. Don't blame him really. He thinks the safest thing to do is euthanasia for all you angels." Silence. "He may have a point."

Maddie flew off his shoulder, onto the back of the couch so that she was staring him eye to eye. Benjamin exclaimed, "Don't look at me like that, Maddie! I'm at my wit's end, and you know what a short trip that was. I may be an old man, but I don't want to die."

Pacing his loft, he muttered, "I have been racking my brains for a solution, but I keep coming up short. Then I keep thinking about other men my age. Plenty of them have bad habits: many smoke, booze it up, eat badly, and don't get any exercise, all potentially deadly habits in the long run. My only hobbies, or habits you might say, have always been my birds and baseball. I haven't been able to play baseball in years, but my birds have always been there for me. Now it has become a game of feathered roulette. One of you may one day be the death of me. I don't like it, but I must live with it; I don't know if I could murder any of my family."

"In any case, never you, my lady fair." He held out his hand to his cloud and smoke colored companion. She hesitantly stepped onto his finger and sighed. A smile broke across his face at her trust, quickly followed by a frustrated groan.

"But what kind of life will the lot of you have? None of you will ever be able to fly freely again. Some insane person got poor Dizzy Dean; any of you would be fair game if you left the apartment. You are all literally grounded. I could not let any of you die out there by yourselves, brutally and painfully slaughtered. No one should ever have to die alone."

Maddie violently fluffed up her feathers and shuddered. Benjamin looked at her with a pained expression on his face. "I'm sorry, Maddie; for a moment I forgot."

"I just don't know what to do," he repeated. Shaking his head he mused, "Well, a decision does not have to be made right now, thank God, so let's just let it lie for now."

Tony awoke in a cold sweat, gasping and trembling. His dreams that night had metamorphosed into twisted scenes straight out of a Hitchcock movie: scores of pigeons grew huge talons and began shredding people, including Tony. He stumbled into the living room and peered out on his balcony at the pigeon coop. To his relief, the three birds rested, heads under wings.

"This is ridiculous; my nerves are not going to take this much longer," he shakily thought. Glancing at the clock, he noted the time: five-seventeen. "Great; I have to get up in less than two hours. No way am I going to go back to sleep now."

Wandering through his apartment, he paused in his kitchen and snapped the light on. Tony then proceeded to sit at the table, in a stupor, aimlessly reviewing in his mind the events of the past few days. His mind kept returning to the phone call he had received from Jeni earlier that night.

After just a moment of pleasant greetings, Jeni's voice began to take on a tearful edge. "I heard about the pigeons being TADS carriers."

"Me too."

"What are you going to do?"

"I don't know," Tony said. Jeni started to talk about her week, trying to cheer Tony up.

He listened to the rest of the conversation only half-heartedly, for his mind was fixated on yet another TADS victim and the knowledge that he could be next. Only one other part of their phone call came sharply into focus.

"... Tony, please get rid of those birds. Its not worth the risk. I love you; I don't want you to get like Uncle Tyler, or worse, to die like Maddie. Go get a blood test. My friend Sue works at a medical lab." She gave him the phone number and address. They said their good-byes.

Now, as he sat at his kitchen table, he replayed that conversation over and over, along with the one in the bar with Benjamin. He knew what he had to do.

The morning's light had started to break through the city's dark haze; with the dawn came the stirrings of the birds. His own trio started gentle cooing and fluttering as they awoke. So peaceful, so harmless they sounded, that for a moment Tony nearly lost his resolve.

He held the memory of his neighbor laid out in her coffin in his mind as he searched for, and found, the bag of birdseed. "It's them or me," he repeated as a mantra as he stepped out onto the balcony. With a silent prayer for their avian souls, Tony opened the bag and poured the seed into the feeding tray.

Their hearty morning appetites made short work of their breakfasts, and the poison made short work of their ability to breath. Tony watched the pigeons' final moments through a film of tears. As the last bird finally ceased moving, the film dissolved into totally blinding torrents; Tony stood before Boston's dawn, crying out into the cold morning air his pain and his loss.

Boston remained silent, not even offering him a handkerchief.

Later, Tony sat at the computer and sent an E-mail.

Subject: Angels
To: Nightingale
From: Esquire

It is five in the morning. The city is silent and I am alone in my apartment for the first time since my parents death.

I feel I have become Death, killing angels entrusted to me and so trusting of me.

They are gone, Jeni, all of them.

I was afraid - pure cowardice. I had no choice. I only wish that those excuses could make how I feel now better. I only hope that Maddie, where ever she is, can forgive me. Maybe someday I will even be able to forgive myself.

I wish that you were here ...

Benjamin continued to watch the news in horror as man moved ever closer to making the feathered angels extinct. The government was unofficially sanctioning the murders by keeping silent. Benjamin turned off the set and retreated to the sanctuary of his fire escape to watch the morning. He sought peace of spirit, cruelly denied him by the angry mutters of the small crowd below him. Seven men, led by his angry neighbor Mike, were approaching his building. Viewing themselves as mighty hunters, they were complaining of the lack of feathered game. One even held the corpse of a brightly colored parrot. Benjamin recognized the bird. It had perched in the window of old Parson's pet shop for the last five years. He surmised correctly that they must have smashed the glass and grabbed the bird.

"Damn butcher's!" Benjamin muttered to himself. He wanted to scream it louder but they were many and he was old. They had clubs and a shotgun. He had a baseball bat Babe Ruth had autographed for him back in the old days. He could not fight them, at least not do it and win.

They settled directly under him on the porch, oblivious to his presence. They broke out the beer in celebration of their "brave" deeds. From the smell, even three stories up, it was easy to tell it was not their first drink of the day.

"Rid the neighborhood of those disease ridden birds, finally," said one.

"Damn killers every one."

"To be honest, I'll miss the little buggers."

"Why?"

"I enjoyed hunting the things. What a rush pounding their brains in. It was healthy. Letting off stress, you know. I just pictured my boss's face on each of them and the rest was easy."

"Yea. I pretended they was my old lady."

"Why, Joey? They wouldn't have sex with you either?" jibed one. Joey hit him on the shoulder.

"Too bad they are all gone. I would enjoy doing a few more."

"Stick to your old lady, Joey."

"Wait, maybe he has a point. Maybe there are more pigeons to kill," Mike suggested.

"Where? New York? I don't feel like no road trip."

"No. Birds right here. In this building," Mike said with an evil grin.

"You mean Benny's birds?"

"Exactly."

"Let the old guy alone. He doesn't hurt anybody. The birds are the only friends he's got left," said Joey.

"Yea, all the other old coots kicked the bucket," laughed Mike.

"Seriously, he has been keeping the birds in his apartment. Leave him be."

"Why? So those birds can poop on my head while I sleep?"

"With your dandruff how would you notice?"

"I am not letting death live above me. I say we kill those stupid birds. Its them or us."

"All right! Lets do it! You coming, Joey?"

"No," said Joey.

"Why the hell not?"

"Cause. Benny's a good guy. When my old man ran off, he used to take me to the Red Sox games. He took most of us at one time or another. I can't do that to him," said Joey.

"So? What has he done for us lately? You have not even said more than ten words at a time to him since you were fifteen. It's just fun. C'mon."

"No."

"Whimp."

"Wussy."

"Whatever. I'm outa here," said Joey, walking off down the street.

"We don't need him. I got the key to the building. We'll sneak upstairs and knock on his door. When the old guy opens it we push it in and grab the pigeons," Mike schemed.

Above, Benjamin heard it all and had a different slant on things. "That's what you think." Within moments and with some small strain Benjamin had the apartment door barricaded with his couch and coffee table. His next step was to dial 911 but he kept getting a busy signal.

He hoped when they did not get an answer that they would give up and go away. No such luck. They were not giving up. Whether it was fear, drink, or dumb macho pride they kept at it. When knocking produced nothing, they moved on to pounding. When that failed they began smashing. The door gave slightly with each blow. If not for the couch it would have burst open by now. 911 was still busy.

That is when the shotgun blast took out the doorknob. A second blast shattered the dead bolt. The couch moved an inch back, then two.

"My God. It is not going to hold!" thought a terrified Benjamin. "Get the hell out of here! I called the police," he yelled, trying to bluff his attackers.

"We will be in and gone before they get here. Just give us the birds and we will not hurt you."

"Never!"

"Have it your way. We are coming in and nothing you can do is going to stop us."

Deep in the pit of his stomach Benjamin knew fear, worse than he had in France during the war. At least then he had a gun and a fighting chance.

Turning to the birds he said "Sorry, kids. There is nothing I can do."

He could set them free, but what chance did they have then? Images from the past few days, of the brutality of the slayings flashed though Benjamin's mind. The pain, the terror the poor dead innocents must have felt. The same was going to happen to his children and he was powerless to stop it. Or was he?

He moved the rarely used kitchen table and a bookcase to strengthen the barricade. He could not stop the mob but he could prevent them from killing his angels. An act of betrayal most foul would save their souls while damning his own. The bag of poisoned seed sang darkly to him. This time he knew the tune he would have to sing. Zombie like, he picked the bag up, looking at Maddie. His expression was one of anguish. His eyes begged for absolution.

"I have to. It is better this way."

Maddie did not argue. Benjamin opened the coops and let the rest of his flock out. Trusting, they flew to the offer of food he held out in his hands as they had so many other times before.

"Eat, my angels, from the hands of your Judas. Soon you will fly to a better place."

They ate. The poison worked quickly. Babe was the first to stumble, then fall. Benjamin held him in his arms weeping.

"I am so sorry, Babe."

Babe breathed his last as Cherub began her last journey. Tenderly Benjamin gathered them up, again whispered his apologies and held then as they died. He did the same for the rest. Mickey... Angel... Joe... Gabriel was the last to go. Benjamin stared into his eyes, tears streaming down his face. Gabriel's eyes showed no anger, only surprise as they closed forever. Benjamin stared at the limp, lifeless forms, so different from the friends he had known for years.

"I did it," sobbed Benjamin, squeezing the departed's bodies close to him in a final embrace, watering their feathers with his tears. Closing his eyes did not stop the flow. Neither did the shudders that racked his body. The pigeons had been his life for many years. Now, they were gone forever. For a moment the pounding of his heart drowned out that of the killers beyond his door. Killers he had now joined the rank of.

"Better they died with me than at the hands of a stranger. At least they did not die alone," he whispered to the still living Maddie, trying desperately to believe his own words. "I never told you, Maddie, but that is my greatest fear. Dying alone."

Maddie bobbed her head consolingly and moved toward the bag of deadly feed.

"No!" Benjamin shouted. "Not you, Maddie. I could not bear to live without you. We will hide you and tell them I killed all my birds. they have no idea how many I have. They will believe me. They have to but just in case..."

Benjamin reached in the refrigerator, took out a full container and began covering himself with the white substance it contained. Once he was adequately shrouded, he turned to Maddie.

"C'mon, we have to hide you. You have to remain perfectly still," Benjamin said, opening up his sock drawer. "This will be cramped but otherwise comfortable."

That was the moment the furniture barricade gave way and the six men outside came crashing in along with the splinters that once were a door.

"Where are the killers?" demanded Mike, waving his shotgun.

"Look in the mirror," suggested Benjamin, gritting his teeth.

"The birds, old man."

"They are taken care of," Benjamin growled, pointing to the tenderly laid out bodies.

"Didn't think you had the balls, old man," said Mike.

"Now get out."

"Are they all dead?"

"Yes."

"Then what are you hiding behind your back?"

"Nothing."

Pushing Benjamin aside, Mike looked at the still open sock drawer. Maddie stared back at him.

"All dead, huh? Then what's that?" demanded Mike.

Benjamin sucker-punched him in the breadbasket, channeling all the anger and hate over what he had been forced to do. Despite his age, he hit hard. Mike buckled to one knee.

"Fly Maddie! Get out of here! Avoid all people!" Benjamin shouted. Maddie looked at him. "I'll be fine. Go!"

Reluctantly Maddie obeyed, flying toward the open window. Mike lifted the shotgun and took aim. Fueled by an extreme of emotion, Benjamin knocked the gun from his hands. Maddie made it to the open skies.

"I'm going to kill you, old man," Mike said, picking up his shotgun and pointing it at Benjamin's midsection.

"Do it... I dare you. At least you will be making sure I won't be going alone."

"Why? You bulletproof or something?"

"Far from it. But a shotgun makes a big mess, especially at close range. My guts will spatter all over you and so will that which you most fear. This," Benjamin said, holding out a handful of the white substance he had covered himself in.

"What is that stuff?"

"Pigeon poop. I have been saving it for you," Benjamin said, smiling as Mike took a giant jump back.

"You crazy? That really pigeon crap?"

"Oh, yes."

"You are sick."

"And you will be soon. I got some on you. But if you go right now and wash it off maybe nothing will happen. You shoot me and you will vaporize some of it. It will fill the air and go into your lungs. Then you will be as good as dead. Your choice."

Mike hesitated briefly before answering. "All right. You won, old man," Mike said as the lot of them left quickly, shaking their heads in disbelief.

Looking around at the remains of his friends and his apartment he said softly "No, I didn't."

Once downstairs, one of the mighty hunters said to Mike "Guess that one got away."

"Not yet, it didn't."

"You gonna sprout wings and chase after it?"

"No, you idiot. It is a homing pigeon. It will come back eventually. All we have to do is wait. We will do it in shifts. Right now I gotta take a shower."

Benjamin spent the morning sneaking around at the Fenway burying his friends and saying a prayer over the shallow grave. Picking up some plywood on the way home, he made a makeshift door. The work kept his mind busy but even busy days have to come to an end. For hours he wept until he ran out of tears. His chest heaved with dry sobs.

Walking to the fire escape, he looked up at the rays of the setting sun. He was oblivious to a drunken Mike and his shotgun lurking below. No one else had bothered to watch with him. He also did not know Tony was a block away and heading toward him.

"Maddie, wherever you are, I pray you are safe."

As if waiting for him, Maddie flew onto his shoulder and began to nuzzle his ear.

"Maddie! You should not have come back! It is too dangerous."

"You don't know the half of it," shouted Mike from below, aiming his gun.

Still half a block away, Tony screamed, "Don't!"

Mike ignored Tony as Benjamin looked down into the muzzle of the gun.

"Say bye-bye, birdie!" snickered Mike, pulling the trigger.

"No!" screamed Benjamin putting himself between the blast and Maddie. It caught him full in the chest. Off balance, he tumbled off the fire escape and down the thirty feet to the street, landing on his back.

"I missed!" muttered Mike drunkenly, getting ready to shoot his second barrel. Tony reached him first, hitting him in the back of the head with his elbow, knocking him down and out.

He rushed to Benjamin's side, cradled his body and was surprised when he heard a moan.

"Benjamin! You are still alive!"

"Barely."

"I always said you were a tough old goat. I'll call an ambulance." Tony instead shouted to a passerby to call, who surprisingly took off running without Tony having to beg. "Lord, I pray he's going for the phone...hang on, Ben."

He took off his coat and pressed it against Benjamin's chest wound in an attempt to stop the bleeding.

"Too late for that, Tony."

"Damn it Ben, why did you do it? It was just a bird."

"Love."

"Love must really be blind. What is this white stuff all over your clothes?"

"Sour cream."

"Why are you covered in it?"

"It is the secret of my youthful complexion," Benjamin said, making a last bitter joke, as his body convulsed in coughing spasms. Turning his head, he spit out a mouthful of blood.

"Take it easy. Don't waste your breath."

"I only have so many left, youngster, and I will waste them as I see fit."

"Yes, sir."

"That's better. Respect for your elders, whether we deserve it or not. I covered myself in the sour cream to convince the barbarians at my door it was pigeon poop so they would leave me alone. Worked great, didn't it?"

"Not especially. Where are the other angels?"

"Dead," Benjamin said, with shame and sorrow, barely able to whisper his final confession. "I killed them so the barbarians couldn't."

"Then why didn't you do the same for Maddie?"

"Couldn't. I never told you. You would have had me locked up for sure...that bird is the real Maddie."

"You are delirious. Rest."

"I'm not going to need rest where I'm going. Maddie!" he called. The bird flew down and landed by his head. Benjamin feebly turned his gaze to her and gently smiled.

"I don't believe it," Tony explained. "She came."

"Of course she did. I told her I was afraid of dying alone. She will stay with me until the end. You will too, won't you?"

"Yes. I will," promised Tony, choking back tears. Desperate to change the subject, he said. "Maddie came to me with your note asking me to come here. Sorry I was too late."

"I didn't write a note."

"But..."

"Was it signed? I doubt it. And it was written by fountain pen, wasn't it? I should thank her. Because of it, I am blessed by your company," Benjamin coughed up even more blood and shivered. "Take care of that girl of yours."

"I will. I was going to tell you..."

"Tell me what?" Benjamin sputtered.

"I 'm asking Jeni to marry me."

"Congratulations, Tony, my boy. Excellent news to end on," Benjamin said.

"End on? No, Ben. Hang on; help is coming. That guy must have called by now."

Benjamin's entire body convulsed in spasms. The jacket was no longer enough to hold back the blood. "Won't matter... it's time. I am going to join Maddie."

"In heaven?"

"More like heaven on Earth. We will be together after all. As angels. Good bye, Tony," Benjamin gasped, reaching up to touch Maddie. It was his last act as his body fell silent.

"Ben? Ben?" asked Tony as a tear trickled down his face. His friend lay still and strangely peaceful. "So long, you old goat. Say hi to Maddie for me."

Mike had regained consciousness and seeing the bird, charged at it, brandishing the shotgun as if it was a club. Maddie flew up to Benjamin's fire escape she perched on it looking down. Mike tripped over Benjamin's body and fell to the ground, dropping the gun.

"Stop it! You already killed a good man. Isn't that enough for you?"

Stumbling to his feet, Mike stammered. "I did not mean to kill him, but he tried to save the bird." His features twisted into a bratty pout. "It was his own fault," he whined.

Too furious for words, Tony reverently laid Benjamin's head down and silently rose to his feet. Walking over to Mike, Tony poured all of his anger and frustration into his clenched fist, speeding straight for the man's chin. Mike's head snapped back, then forward, his eyes staring ahead blankly as he fell backward into a pile of garbage.

From out of the rubbish, a second pigeon arose, a gray-brown one; it flew up to the fire escape where Maddie was waiting. Landing beside her, they nuzzled each other as if embracing. Turning their gaze downward, each seemingly fluttered a single wing farewell toward Tony, who numbly waved back in disbelief, as he witnessed the impossible scene.

Soaring up together, they sped heavenward, wings almost touching, reveling in freedom and love. Their urban flight lasted until, as one, they disappeared into the sunset's fading brilliance.

FLOCK TOGETHER

Subject: Benjamin
To: Nightingale
From: Esquire

Jeni,

I wish I had your number at the hospital. I need to talk. Call me the moment you get in.

It is about Benjamin... There is no easy way to say this. He's dead. You know, I miss him already. He was one hell of a guy.

I stopped by to see your friend Sue about taking the blood test for TADS to calm both our fears. When I came home, Ben's bird, Maddie, was at my apartment, waiting for me with a note. It urged me to get over to his place..

I went, but got there too late. One of the pigeon killers shot Ben in the chest with a shotgun. Ben was trying to protect Maddie. Remember how he always used to talk about believing and how I thought he was loony? We talked as he was dying in my arms and I saw something that I know is impossible but you know what?... I believe. My turn to be loony. I pray he has gone to a better place.

I made a citizens arrest. I'm going to make sure Ben's killer pays.

The funeral is the day after tomorrow. I know you can't come, so don't worry about trying to make it. I just need to talk. Call me as soon as you get in.

I love you.

> Forever,
> Tony

Tony grieved. Looking back on his life it seemed that was all he did. First his parents, killed so stupidly by a drunk. Seventeen is too young to become a real adult, the kind with real responsibility. Maddie took him in and had helped him get through that part of his life. She inspired him to decide what he needed to do with his life. She helped him create his dream of helping the underdog. There were too many people the system was stomping on because no one was there who cared to defend them. He would be that one, a lawyer on a white stallion.

Before she could see him reach that goal, Maddie died so senselessly, victim of an invisible virus which made her own world her enemy. Without her, Tony was left truly alone, without anyone looking out for him. Without anyone to look out for. Except the birds.

Before his parents died they let him get Raphael, his first bird. Maddie helped him train it. He would go on public transportation, rides with friends and strangers, just to give Raphael a place to fly home from. When that bird took to the heavens, he carried Tony's spirit with him. Part of him liked to believe Maddie's stories that they were really angels. It made him special, to have his own angel.

Maddie left him two of her angels, to watch over and be watched over by. He had something to focus on, training them to recognize his balcony as home, instead of hers. It took the people who bought Maddie's condo some time to get used to the pigeons landing on their balcony. Not to mention Tony constantly knocking on their door to retrieve them. Eventually it became a joke. With time, Wings and Michael had learned. Every time they flew, it was like Maddie was not dead, at least for those few moments.

He never did figure out Maddie the bird, at least until it was too late. The explanation was too incredible. It still was, but now he believed, despite his better sensibilities.

Now all his angels were dead, victims of TADS as surely as Maddie was. Not only did he grieve for the birds, but he punished himself for becoming their executioner. He knew it had to be done, that he was right. That did not make him feel any better.

Lastly, there was Benjamin. He started correspondence with the old goat mostly as an obligation to Maddie. That and an excuse to fly the birds. Benjamin was the only person he knew with the same passion. It was a bond, small at first, but it grew.

Benjamin appeared gruff, but was all heart. Always could tell from the letters if Tony was in a bad mood. Tried to cheer him up. Encouraged him with his classes which Tony desperately needed when things got hectic, .

They had an unspoken agreement not to let the Maddie situation recreate itself and had met every month or two. Once, when Tony had been very ill with the flu, and Jeni had been home visiting her folks, Benjamin made the trek up through a Boston snow storm to bring him chicken soup. Thankfully, he had bought it at a nearby deli and not made it himself.

Benjamin also became a sounding board for his relationship with Jeni. For a life long bachelor, he had excellent advice. Ben claimed he simply looked back at what he had done in the past and advised Tony to do the opposite.

He still saw that final scene. It played over and over in his mind, in his dreams. The blast, then the fall. Tony always wondering if he had been a minute earlier, could he have saved Benjamin?

Tony took special interest in the murder case and was going to make sure the gunman did not get off easy. The baser side of him wondered if he should have hit the gunman more, harder - maybe hard enough to make sure he never got up again. The part of him that was his soul knew he did what was right. To do otherwise would have been to shame the memories of those whom he loved, living and dead, two of which he was no longer sure how to classify.

If he himself had killed, in jail there could be no Jeni and that would have been his personal hell. No matter how bad things got, Jeni was there for him. Her power, love, and humor could make him forget the pain. Together, he often told her, they could take on the world.

It was time to make it permanent. Benjamin was the only one he told, other than the jeweler who resized his mother's engagement ring.

"Mother would have loved Jeni. If only..." Tony mused.

He had been getting too morbid. One thing that he loved to do as a kid was make prank phone calls. It had gotten him grounded more than once, but that did not stop him. It only slowed him down. It was time to relive part of childhood in preparation for his night of nights.

The phone rang. Roy looked at it strangely. The phone never rang at this hour. It was his time to relax, after all the graves had been dug and the newly occupied ones filled in.

He debated about not answering it but it might be his boss, checking up on him. The same boss that was too cheap to buy him an answering machine to take messages. After the fifth ring, he decided the caller would not be giving up, so he resigned himself to his fate.

Roy answered the phone. "St. Jude Cemetery."

"Roy, is that you?" Tony asked, a sly smile on his face.

"Yes. Who is this?" Roy asked confused.

"Yes, indeedy," Tony said, purposely evading the question. "As I am sure you know, I am calling regarding a matter of grave importance," The pun flew right over

Roy's head. "I just got off the phone with your boss. He said you were the man who could answer this question for me. I'm sure your boss has talked to you, has he not?" Tony led and lied.

"Sure, ...um, I think," Roy stammered, confused.

"Excellent. Now what I need to know is will there be any open graves, awaiting burial, tomorrow?"

"One. Why?"

"Your boss was supposed to explain that all to you. Are you telling me he lied to me?"

Not wanting to get in trouble, Roy answered "Oh, he did tell me. It just took me a minute to remember is all."

"Glad to hear it. Now what is the plot number and general location?"

"N124, to the left just inside the south gate and 12 rows down, five plots in."

"Got it. And what time will you be there until, in case I have any more questions?"

"Five thirty."

"Same tomorrow?"

"Yes."

"Splendid. I would like to make a reservation for two."

"Excuse me?"

"And please leave your wine list out."

"What are you talking about? This is a graveyard, not a restaurant."

"Indeed it is. You have been quite helpful. Ta, ta," Tony said, hanging up.

The fatigue that had been overwhelming him of late was temporarily lifted. He was full of vigor. Everything had to be perfect. He would meet Jeni at their old favorite diner. He had double checked the weather report. It was to be a clear evening with a full moon. He had resized his mother's ring and ordered the flowers. He had his speech prepared and memorized. There was one last item on the list. Where could he find a ladder?

Being someone who disliked attracting attention, Tony tried to maintain a low profile as he purposefully strode through the crosswalk, ladder under arm. However, the sight of a well-suited man with a six-foot paint-splattered ladder and a dozen long-stemmed roses was a bit unusual. Several young tag-a-longs were cheerfully calling out:

"Where ya goin'?... what'ca doin'?...". One boy who had apparently watched a few comedies on elopements, manfully declared, "I bet he's gonna 'lop with his girl...right, mister?"

Tony fought between just ignoring the group or grinning in agreement. As he neared his destination, the boy in him whispered the alternative. Without breaking stride, he looked over his shoulder and, with a terrible frown, growled, "I'm going to the cemetery to see my brother."

"What's the ladder for?" asked a brown-haired girl, with a hint of fear in her voice.

"We're burying him today and I'm going to climb down in the pit to say goodbye one last time." Tony could hear the sudden halt of footsteps behind him, followed by a noisy retreat of his followers. He quietly chuckled, and made a brisk left turn down the last block to the diner.

His silent mirth was interrupted by the "beep, beep, beep" of his pager. Of course, it was hooked on the side directly under the ladder. Cursing, he awkwardly leaned his burden against a post, and glanced down at the offending box.

He stopped, feeling strangely numb as he recognized Jeni's friend Susie's work number. A part of him wanted desperately to pretend that the call had not been placed. But he could not run from reality. After scanning the number, he searched for and miraculously found a working phone booth.

Minutes later, Tony's world was forever overturned.

He placed the receiver on its hook, and stood mute, eyes searching his surroundings as if never seen before. He slid his hand into his coat pocket and surrounded its contents, gripping it as if it were his lifeline out of his present sinking circumstances. After a time of ponderings, he released his grip and instead, gathered up the flowers and ladder. With a set mouth and swimming eyes, he proceeded to where he was meeting Jeni.

"Tony certainly was doing his best to keep me in the dark regarding what's going on tonight," Jeni mused as she stared past her seatmate's florid nose at the passing scenery. At least she had time to guess the evening's plans on her trip from New York. The woman seemed lost in her own mind's ramblings and had not uttered a word the entire time, save for a muttered "'scuse" when she had unceremoniously belched a time or two.

Jennifer pulled out a neatly folded sheet from her jacket's pocket. Unfolding it, she reread the E-mail Tony had sent to her last night. She had not read it until she had gotten off her shift around 7 this morning. Her face softened into a gentle smile as she reread the note.

Subject: @->>> - (rose) and <<<HUGS>>> X
          infinity..
To: Nightinggale
From: Esquire

I trust that your bags are packed and waiting for
you by your front door; I know I've been waiting for
you since your last visit....too long! :) :)

As this is our first anniversary, I have PLANS!
When you get off the train, catch the subway stop
near your old apartment. There, await further in-
structions.

I shall arrive at 6:00 sharp. Be prepared to be
wined, dined, and amazed.

With love and impatience,
"Hey you"

She glanced at her watch; she was cutting it close -
about 45 minutes until they were to meet. Thank God the
train seemed to be on time; she could feel it slowing down
for her stop.

Minutes later, she was frantically waving down a taxi
and heading for her destination. "Going to make it OK,"
she settled into the back seat smiling.

But thanks to the usual snarled traffic, she arrived late;
but only by about five minutes. Entering the little corner
diner, she slipped her bag and herself into the booth that
she and Tony had claimed as "ours" by virtue of the many
hours spent there.

After she had finished her glass of ice water and spent
some time playing stack-up with the sugar packets, she
began to wonder what was keeping Tony. Promptness was
definitely not one of his strong points today; by her watch,
he was about 20 minutes late. She mentally shook her
head with mock disapproval; she was usually the one that

kept him waiting. And anyway, how could she fuss today? She rose from the table and with her bag, strolled outside to wait for him. People were flowing by her on their own paths and she leaned against the wall, peering through them, searching for his face.

"Hey, Jeni!"

She turned to see Tony parting the crowds like Moses, carrying a ladder and a bouquet of flowers. The sight caused her to giggle like a ticklish ten-year-old.

"What's THAT for?" Her eyes grew wide as it dawned on her. "We are not going to do what I think we are, are we?"

"Well, if you think that we are going hunting for bird nests...no."

His face held a huge grin, but as he came closer, she could not help noticing that his eyes did not match the rest of his face: they seemed lost in thought, and reddened as if he were holding back tears.

Should she question him, she pondered. No, better to just wait and see if he says anything.

"Sorry that I'm late," he said as he breathlessly came to a stop beside her. "Happy anniversary, sweetheart." He presented to her the roses with a flourish, and kissed her as well as he could holding a ladder.

"I called Grandmama's restaurant to deliver here in about ...mmm..." he checked his watch, "...ten minutes or so."

"I bet the person that took your order about died when you gave the address."

Tony's chuckle seemed almost absent-minded....yep, she thought, there is something definitely wrong going on. She was determined to wait for him to talk.

Jeni laughingly asked, "And pray tell, where are we going to picnic, sir? If you are going for nostalgia, the hole we met in has been occupied for a year now."

Tony shrugged. "Well, I admit that we can't exactly

recreate the scenario, but I did find out that there is a very attractive little "basement" property just past the entrance facing the commons...will that do?"

"Lets go check it out. Here, let me grab an end."

Each one held on to the ladder as they proceeded to the cemetery.

As they passed through the gate, Tony finally looked at her, eye to eye, and almost whispered, "Have I told you yet how much I love you?"

"Not yet today...Tony, is everything OK?" although she had decided not to question him, her concern overwhelmed her discipline. She searched his face for an explanation to his "off" mood.

Tony turned away and slightly stiffened. "Nah, just a bad morning; nothing so important that can't wait until later. Sorry my mood's so obvious, Hon...I just want everything to be perfect today."

As they approached the plot, they saw not an open grave but a freshly packed mound covered with flowers. This sight seemed to be the last straw for Tony.

A moan escaped his lips as they came up to the grave. "No...damn, damn, damn... it's not fair!" He dropped his part of the ladder and brought his hands up to his face, hiding it.

"Tony, its OK, really," Jennifer tried to comfort. "That caretaker must have beaten us to the punch. They must have upped the time for the ceremony. Tony," she continued, "It doesn't matter... we're together, that's all I want now."

As if to change the subject, a slightly confused-looking girl pushing a bike with a "Grandmama's Delivery" saddlebag draped across it approached them.

"Uhh... excuse me, sir; are you Tony Jordan?"

"Yes, he is," Jennifer quickly answered for him, as he appeared to be only slightly aware of the intruder.

"This may sound strange, but I have a delivery for him

here." She reached into her bags and brought out several Styrofoam containers, paper bags, and a bottle of wine. "This was charged, I just need his signature."

Tony signed the slip and, after tipping her, watched the girl hop on her bike and rapidly pedal out of the cemetery. Jennifer peeked in a large bag and exclaimed, "Yum, fresh French bread...I'm starved! Where do you want to consume this stuff, Tony?"

He tried a smile. "I was going to recite 'a loaf of bread, a jug of wine, and thou', but I'm no poet. I...." He struggled to continue, but the tears wouldn't let him.

"Tony, honey, what is wrong? It can't be this?"

He stood here, silently struggling for a moment, then quietly said, "Sue beeped me on the way over here."

Jennifer felt a chill envelope her; she forced the words out through fear-clenched teeth. "What are the results?"

"Positive. I'm assuming stage one, since I don't have any acute symptoms."

Jennifer switched into her practical nursing mode. "The tests don't diagnosis the stage, just the presence of the virus. Based on your age and past health history, you have several months if you're careful and they start a broad spectrum antibiotic program before you have to go in....." She faltered, knowing his fate. "Oh, Tony!"

"Yeah," he replied. "Oh, me!" He looked at her with such intense longing. "Today I wanted this to be such a special, wonderful day...I wanted to take you in my arms and tell you how much you mean to me...I'm so sorry."

"Sorry? Tony, I know you care; right now I'm terrified for you and I'm terrified that I'm going to lose you."

"Jeni, regardless, you will never lose my love, it is Evermore." They hugged one another tightly, crushing the aborted feast between them. He reached into his pocket and clutched the ring. "As for a future for us together... you know better than anyone else what would be ahead of us."

Jennifer slowly said. "Tony, what are you trying to say?"

"I'm saying that sticking with me would not be fair to you. I'm saying that when I go into a bubble I want you to start dating others, try to go on with your life." As Jennifer was staring at him in fear, pain, and shock, he exploded. "Damn it, Jeni, I'm trying to be noble about this. Please don't make this even harder."

The tears came fiercely now from both of them. As he pulled away, her hold on his arm caused him to drop the small jewelry case. Before he could react, Jennifer reached down and picked it up. She opened it and gently slid the ring onto her finger.

"The answer is yes," she said with a new-found strength.

"I didn't ask the question," he protested.

"But you were going to ..."

"This changes everything..."

"Not where it counts. Tony, I love you, and I will gladly say those vows 'in sickness and in health'. I will take any time given to us. And who knows, I haven't been tested; I may have..."

"No! I can't even think of that. You can't have this." He stood, mind racing and confused, heart torn and soul empty. "I have to think, I can't deal with everything; all this is going to change. I have to go for a walk...get away." He fumbled with his wallet and held out some money. "Here, Jeni, take a cab to the apartment. I promise to be there later; I've got to be by myself for awhile. Please understand."

As she did not move, he let the bills drift to the ground amidst the picnic's wreckage. Picking up the ladder, he cradled it under his arm and stood there, "The ring looks wonderful on you, please keep it; it belongs to you." She clasped her other hand over the ring and stared pleadingly at him.

"I do love you," he declared. She watched him go, ladder bouncing against his side, looking almost comical except for her knowledge of the pain within him and the tears glistening in both their eyes.

Three hours had passed, and Tony had not returned to the apartment. Jeni had been pacing the length of the place for most of the hours until she was becoming positively claustrophobic. Her confinement just continued to remind her how Tony would feel living his life out in one of those bubbles, and how alone she would feel without him. The rhythm of her feet mockingly pounded out .."in- u -en-DO, in -u - en- DO". Finally, she collapsed on the couch .

Jeni was at once level-headed and frantic. There was a way; she just needed to find it is all. A cure was out of her power. Therefore, she needed a way into the bubble herself.. Maybe she could get a job as a nurse? No, then she would have to wear an E-suit and they still would be unable to touch. How to keep the two of them together?

Then it came to her. She reached for the phone and dialed up her friend at the medical lab.

"Sue, this is Jeni. Tony told me the results of the test....no, he's not taking it well at all; neither am I, if you want to know the truth."

She listened for a moment to Sue's condolences, then took a very deep breath and with eyes closed in prayer, asked, "Listen, Sue...what I have to ask is very, very important to me... Remember when I helped you write that term paper that you needed to graduate and you said if I ever needed a favor, just ask? I am asking now: I need your help with a blood test."

"I don't care, Sue... I am not going to be separated

from him. This is the only way...I know I have my whole life in front of me. It is my life and I'll live it as I want to...please?"

After much argument, Sue finally agreed to Jeni's plan. Jeni agreed to wait a week or two before springing the plan, to give time for any alternatives to be thought of. Sue would make sure Jeni's test was positive and if they married before entering, she and Tony would be together. Jeni said her good-byes, and sat, phone in hand, going over her plan in her mind.

They had to be placed in the same bubble, Jeni worried, otherwise, the ruse was worse than useless. "This has to work," she muttered.

"What has to work, Jeni?"

Tony's near voice startled Jeni so, she dropped the phone. "Tony! Don't scare me like that." She quickly recovered and embraced him. "Are you OK? I've been so worried."

He held her close, almost whispering apologetically. "After I dropped the ladder off, I walked for a bit, then rode the subway around." He gave a grim little smile. "I was really hoping someone would try to mug me so I could beat the crap out of them. I was so angry, I needed a target, you know?" She nodded.

"Wouldn't you know-everyone was on their best behavior. Where's a gang member when you need one?" She felt his shoulders sag in despair. "I feel so helpless, Jeni," he moaned.

They sat on the couch, consoling one another, until the dawn greeted them as it did one year ago, together.

Tony was surprised to find himself at the funeral parlor, viewing Benjamin's body. He could smell the roses and other assorted flowers cluttering the room. But Ben was not in his blue suit that he was buried in; instead, he had on his usual ratty brown pants and beige shirt. As Tony hesitantly approached the casket, the body was suddenly covered in white, creamy-looking globs.

"Its just sour cream...didn't work, did it?" Ben turned and winked at him. "Maddie!" he called out, arm outstretched.

A huge white pigeon flew into the room, wings fanning the flowers into a storm of multi-colored petals. As it landed on Ben's hand, it metamorphosed into the real Maddie, face shining with love. She cradled her cheek in Ben's palm, as he sat up in the casket. "My angel," he beamed. He shook a scolding finger at Tony. "You take care of your angel, son."

As they embraced, the figures shifted: Tony was witnessing Benjamin standing over Maddie, so still and calm on her deathbed. Tony's eyes stung with remembered tears over his surrogate aunt. As the tears caused the scene to blur, an avalanche of faces fought for space in the coffin: his parents, the older couple, even a friend from his junior high days that had died.

Tony began to feel ill; vertigo was overtaking him. His own face stared at him from the mahogany box. Maddie's hands were cradling his face, gently rocking him from side to side.

"Tony, love is Evermore... Evermore... Tony... Evermore..."

"Tony, love, wake up."

Tony felt Jennifer's hands lightly touching his cheeks. He opened one eye, and was greeted by Jenny's concerned but loving stare.

"You were having a nightmare; are you all right?"

"Uh-huh," he grunted. "All mixed up: Ben, and Maddie, my mom and dad...it was crazy, but I'm awake now. Thanks."

They kissed tenderly good-morning and Tony knew the message the dream was showing him. "I love you," he declared.

"I love you, 'hey you'," she grinned. She pulled on his arm. "I want to show you something I saw out the window; I hope that it is still there. C'mon!"

They went to the window and peered out. "Look!" she exclaimed.

Pigeons. There weren't many left, thanks to the slaughtering times, but a few defiantly remained. They danced in the rising sun's flames, dipping up and down as if surfing on crimson waves. There were close to a dozen, too far away to make out colors. Tony wondered if Maddie and Ben were among them.

"They are so beautiful," Jennifer sighed.

"What a wonderful view to wake up to," he agreed. "Where there is life, there's hope."

"Exactly," Jennifer said. "Well, lively - let's go get breakfast."

Tony stretched hugely, dropping his arms about her. After a hug, he said, "I think we need to change first, grunge went out a long time ago."

She looked down at her wrinkled clothes and mugged. "We do look like a couple of homeless people, don't we?"

"Yep, go shower; ladies first."

She replied with a twinkle in her eye. "Well, I doubt I qualify as a lady, but who am I to turn down the first shot at the hot water - bye." She grabbed her bag by the couch and bolted for the bathroom door. Turning, she shook her finger playfully at Tony. "Stay awake, now."

"I promise; save some hot water for me."

"No promises," Jeni stuck her tongue out at him and disappeared through the door.

Tony quickly grew contemplative. How could he live

without her? He noticed the ring was still on her finger; the sight of it there gave him quiet pleasure. What could they do....

He realized that in less than two weeks he was due to take his bar exam - great, he groaned, nothing like an additional stress to add to his present situation. Why even bother when within months he was going to bottled up forever.

As he sat thinking about it further, he began to realize that having a law degree might be a definite advantage. It depended on how scarce lawyers were in the bubble population. He needed to make some calls.

Going over to his computer, he logged on and went into the phone directory. Keying in TADS Treatment Centers, he was presented with a list of numbers. Narrowing them down to those on the east coast, USA, he hit Print and sat back, waiting. This action gave him some control over the situation; he felt almost good. He would call them later today.

Listening to Jennifer's singing in the shower, he shouted. "Hey Nightingale; quit warbling in there and save me some water, never mind hot!" A very loud and wet raspberry answered him, but the water did shut off. Within a short time, a dressed but slightly damp Jennifer emerged.

"Spoil-sport," she pouted. Tony laughed, nodding in agreement.

As they passed, he grabbed her elbow. Looking very serious, he said. "I don't want to discuss my problem anymore until tonight, OK? I just want to enjoy being with you today."

"I promise not to bring it up, Tony, but we do have to talk about it later. It won't go away....and neither will I."

He gave her arm a squeeze. "Thank you."

She shrugged. "Nothing to thank me about; it is my pleasure," she stated impishly. "In sickness and in health, you know." As he started to protest, she held her hand up. "Uh, uh, uh; no talking about it , you said."

He rolled his eyes,"I better choose my statements more carefully; some lawyer I'm going to make."

She looked at him with determination. "I have no doubt that you will make a damn fine lawyer." Then, the twinkle returned. "But if not, you have other talents."

He bowed. "Thank you, my dear. You can list them to me over breakfast. Right now, the water awaits."

"Have fun," she waved. He turned, and both said, "Yep, a keeper."

Giggling, Jennifer said, "OK, enough mutual admiration society...go!" He went.

A week later, Tony told Jennifer: he was not going to take the bars in Boston, but in Richmond, Virginia. Apparently he had been checking out bubble centers that were in need of legal advice; several already had in-house lawyers, a few others did not seem interested in having any. But Richmond was one of four that were willing to take him in exchange for discounting his admission and maintenance fees. Virginia boards were in three days and he needed to fly down.

"Since your uncle is already scheduled to be transferred there, I figure that it would be the most logical choice. That way you can visit both of us when you want to."

"Tony, I have some news of my own..... "

Jennifer did not have Sue do the tests directly; she knew that Tony would suspect trickery immediately if she had done that. But Sue herself had a friend who owed her a favor or two, so it was a relatively easy matter.

At her comment, Tony turned visibly pale.

"Sweetheart, please don't tell me what I think you're going to...you don't have TADS too, do you?" She silently nodded yes. "Jeni, if this is a joke, it's not funny."

"No joke, I've got it too." She quickly continued. "If we are to stay together, we are going to have to marry soon, otherwise they might put us in separate places." She shuddered at the thought. "I'm sure that Richmond would welcome a nurse as well."

As he silently stared at her, with sorrow and pain painted with broad strokes across his face, Jennifer decided that it was time to take charge. Reaching into her fanny pack, she pulled out a small box.

"I know that men as a rule don't have engagement rings, but you know that I don't usually follow rules anyway." She held out the box to him, opening the lid. "I gave you my answer already; now I am asking you - Tony, will you marry me?"

Tony slowly picked up the ring. It was a thick gold band, with flying birds encircling it. Inside was engraved: "Our love rides on the wings of angels."

Looking up from the ring, he smiled. "Looks like I'm outnumbered - my common sense vs. you and my heart. Yes, my only love, I will marry you."

Before she could embrace him, Tony's smile widened and he reached into his pocket. Pulling out a small wrapped box, he said. "After your present, mine is not much. That day I was gone for a few hours, I came upon a peddler's cart that had something that I thought you would like. I've been saving it for the right time; I guess this is the best time."

When Jennifer saw what was inside the box, she gasped, "Maddie's!", for inside was a crystal heart with an engraved figure of a flying bird.

"I got it from the same guy that Ben did."

"It is the most wonderful present you could give me." She slipped it around her throat. "I love you, Tony."

"I love you," he replied as they embraced, temporarily hiding the heart between them. As their kiss ended, Tony sighed.

"If we both didn't have TADS, I would say that we have heaven on earth; with you, I feel that we can beat anything."

A fleeting moment of guilt washed over her, but she tried to brush the memory of her deceit aside. "All anyone has is one day at a time, hon. We have that... I'm happy for that."

"Mom, Dad: I have some good news and some bad news...." Jennifer felt as if she was trapped in the middle of a bad joke with an awful punchline. Her parents were thrilled about the engagement, but when she told them that she was infected - she was realizing how many people her little lie was affecting.

Her mother took the news with a quiet moan of despair, but her father answered her announcement by slamming his fist through the living room wall, requiring them all to take him to the emergency room for X-rays. The shock of his reaction terrified Jennifer - her father was not by nature a violent man. Her words had driven him into a rage at his inability to protect his little girl this time in her life. His pain tore deeply at her.

All the way to the ER, she fought to keep from taking back her words; tears kept leaking from everyone's eyes, hers included. Her lie kept growing larger as she had to answer questions about her symptoms and present health. How was she going to continue this charade for the duration?

"Don't worry about Zeus, dear," her mother said. "I promise that we will take good care of him."

"Zeus? Oh, m'god! I didn't even think about the big goof." No more daily romps? No more evenings, curled up on the couch, fighting for the last popcorn kernel? "Thanks, Mom. I know you all will." She felt as if she was losing her best friend.

Lying to Tony was by far the worst part; how could she lie to someone she loved so much? "I'm doing this for both our sakes." She kept rationalizing to herself.

But she knew in her heart that a day of reckoning was approaching: They were scheduled to enter the TADS center's quarantine area in nine days, their wedding was to be ASAP: as in nine days. After much discussion between themselves and the center, it was decided that they would have the wedding at the center, in the visiting area, just prior to entering the mandatory two week quarantine.

The center looked upon it as a PR opportunity; Jeni wanted it there so that her Uncle Tyler could be there. As he had been in the hospital, he would not have to go through a lengthy holding period as she and Tony would. He would travel straight from the hospital to the center wearing an E-suit, which prevented contamination.

The suit would allow Tyler to attend the wedding. In keeping with the public air of the wedding, the center was going to let him use the E-suit, so they could demonstrate for the media and audience how safe transportation of the Innuendoes was. All Uncle Tyler had to do was to pay for his transportation costs there and back to the hospital, since he would not be moving into the center then; the future residents were to be sent there all together, as the center still needed some necessary last-minute work.

A quiet groan from behind her broke her train of thought, returning her to the present problem.

"How's your hand, Dad?" Her father sat hunched in the back seat, cradling his injured wrist.

He sheepishly replied, "It's all right, dear. Just my luck to hit a stud; if it was just the drywall, I wouldn't have gotten hurt - that much. I just lost it... I wish I could do something to help...."

"Just love me, Dad - that's all." She reached over and squeezed her mother's hand. "You too, Mom. I'll be fine - really. Tony has managed to get both of us into Cheshire House..."

"So at least the two of you will be with Tyler... that's good," her mother optimistically said.

After that, the conversation faltered. Each person sat among their own thoughts, awaiting their arrival at the hospital, each wondering how they would make it through the rest of this day, the rest of this life.

"Jeni, though I would love for us to be together, I really didn't have this scenario in mind." Uncle Tyler was trying to be his usual upbeat self at the news, but this time his performance was not convincing. He raised his hands, placing them on the glass and mimed clasping his niece's and Tony's hands. "But I must admit that a very selfish part of me is glad that the two of you will be able to be there with me."

"It took a lot of negotiating on my part," Tony said. "But having both of us licensed already was helpful."

"Wha...back up; when did you graduate, Jeni?"

"I was already finished with clinicals, and was able to take my board exams ahead of my class for hardship reasons. I was lucky they were able to bend the rules a bit." She gave her uncle a small grin. "And I already have a job...a lifetime contract as Cheshire House's resident RN," She hugged Tony. "Tony has agreed to work as their lawyer. His board results haven't come back yet, but the center is taking him based on his school record."

Tony shrugged, "I'm probably the world's lowest paid

lawyer: just room and board."

"And life, my boy, and there is no price tag on that."
Tyler looked solemnly at the couple, and promised. "It
will be OK, kids; you have Uncle Tyler here on your side
and I will try to make your new lives as easy as possible."

"'New lives' is the right term; we're truly starting a
new life together, both as a couple and as Innuendoes."
Tony gave Jeni a soft kiss and sighed.

"Ugh... I hate that terms...makes me sound sneaky or
something," Tyler grimaced, then grinned. "I do want to
warn you that there is no honeymoon suite. It is commu-
nity living, barracks style at the hospital, but Cheshire
House is much bigger. Hopefully, it will be better there,
but I doubt there will be many private rooms."

"The director told us all about the center's operations,
and assured us that if they ever went to all-dormitory
arraignments, it would only be a temporary situation until
the excess population could be moved to other centers."

"I hope that doesn't happen.. I hope they find a cure for
this before it ever gets to that," Tyler stated.

'I've got to tell Tony.' Jennifer agonized silently.

"Uncle Tyler, are conversations here taped?" she
asked.

This question startled Tyler. "Why no, I don't think so.
The hospital tries to give us as much privacy as the
circumstances permit. What is it?"

She sat, picking at her nails and fidgeting as she tried
to arrange the words in her mind just right. "You both
must promise not to make a scene... it is very important; it
could blow everything. Promise?" Both men warily nodded. "Now remember...keep it quiet....." she softly said.
"My test result was negative."

At first, Tyler was confused as to what test she was
talking about, but Tony exploded. "What!!!!!" It was....."

Jennifer slapped her hand across his mouth and hissed
"Hush! They're watching us," The attendants were staring

curiously at the trio. "Now," she continued, "Let's talk about this very softly or we'll not only get kicked out of here, we might not be allowed to live together." Tony's eyes widened at her statement. He nodded, and she removed her hand.

At the point, Tyler got it. "TADS?" he whispered. Jennifer shrugged her shoulders upward and mouthed 'yes'. Tyler grunted, "Uh-huh!" The attendants looked away. Turning to Tony, he remarked, "This woman sure loves you, Tony."

"If you tell Tony, they will not let me be with you. Don't you want us to be together?" Jeni added.

"Yes, but..." Tony tried to inject.

She interrupted with a rush. "This is the only way. This will not ruin my life: I will have you; I will have my profession; I will still have my family. I am giving up nothing; I am gaining all that I ever wanted. I have thought this out . Is there any objection that you might have that I missed?"

Tony sputtered incoherently at her discourse. Tyler remarked. "She's got you out-maneuvered, Tony. I think you had better give up - are you sure you're the lawyer?"

Tony threw up his arms in defeat. He asked Tyler, "Has she always been so stubborn in getting her way?"

Tyler nodded. "Get used to it, my good man. She can be a handful."

Jennifer laughed. "Thanks uncle, but I'm worth it - right, Tony?"

Tony embraced her. "You are worth everything, Jeni."

"Good, discussion closed," she announced, feeling wonderful .

"Lord, help me," Tony moaned playfully.

"I think that he already has, by giving you two each other," Tyler said.

The wedding party was small, only twenty or so, but the press more than made up for the size of the group; there must have been thirty or forty news people, mostly tabloids, covering the "First Innuendo Wedding". Fittingly, the ceremony took place in a hall where one wall was nothing but window. A sign of times to come.

After her confession weeks ago, a burden felt lifted off Jennifer's heart; now she could go through with the ceremony. Standing beside Tony, she looked up at him, admiring his profile. Her only regret was that Zeus was not the ring bearer. She had come up with the idea and Tony agreed, but her mother had outright refused to have a dog in the wedding party. Jeni had begged and pleaded, but her mother steadfastly prohibited the dog's attendance, threatening not to attend. To keep peace, Jeni conceded.

"Dearly beloved..."

Jeni's father, Mr. Robbins, stood proudly, unable to help himself from crying over how beautiful his little girl looked. His wife nudged him ever so slightly with her elbow. People were watching. He waved her off but did take the handkerchief she offered. Mrs. Robbins had two. The second she kept for herself.

Uncle Tyler was standing at attention, surrealistically dressed up in a self-contained environmental suit and was grinning broadly at her through the visor. When Jeni glanced over at him, he gave them a vigorous thumbs-up sign. He was holding Zeus on a leash. Somehow, he had gotten someone to bring the dog and put a dickey and bow tie on him. It matched the one Tyler had put on outside his E-suit. Jennifer and Tony both fought to keep from giggling. "Every damn time he makes me laugh, even during my own wedding," Jeni thought silently.

Tony did not mind the dog's presence at all; however, Jeni's mother was having a conniption. Jeni looked at Tony but only started to giggle harder. Instead, they turned to face forward and fought to keep a straight face. They each squeezed the other's hands.

It was time to speak their heartfelt vows. They wrote some of the vows themselves but one line they refused to change.

"...in sickness, and in health, ..."

The priest asked for the rings. Tony did not turn to the best man. Instead, he spun to face the congregation, specifically Tyler and Zeus. Tyler was placing a lace covered mini-shopping bag in the dog's mouth and pointing him toward the makeshift alter.

Mother and daughter whispered in unison, "What is he doing?" - one happily, the other mortified.

Mr. Robbins chose not to answer Mrs. Robbins, staring forward with all his might, barely suppressing a grin.

Tony choose to answer Jeni. "Tyler wanted to get you a gift. He could not exactly go shopping so when he heard about your wish he took it upon himself to get Zeus here to carry the rings."

"You knew about this?" Jeni asked amazed.

"He checked with your father and me to make sure you would not mind," Tony answered.

"Daddy?"

"Yep. Just don't tell your Mom. Tyler said he would take all the heat. Now call the mutt."

Jeni bent down on both knees and the photographers, both wedding and media, moved into place. Jeni then slapped her thighs. Zeus, bag in mouth, romped over to her. Jeni removed the bag, handed it to Tony and hugged and kissed Zeus. Jeni motioned to her Uncle to come up to the alter and she handed him Zeus' leash. She whispered "Thanks." and, moving her veil, kissed the 'cheek' of his helmet.

"Great," Tyler said sarcastically. "You got lipstick on my visor. I can't see anything."

Jeni smiled and silently motioned him to stand on the

far end of the line of ushers with Zeus. The media loved it. Great visuals and a sound bite. Even Mrs. Robbins was smiling, waiting for a better time to have a "discussion" with Tyler.

Rings and promises of love were exchanged, each with a single "I do," and the ceremony reached its joyous conclusion.

"I pronounce you husband and wife. You may kiss the bride."

Tony raised the white veil off Jeni's face and kissed her like he had kissed her so many months before, when they were trapped deep in the Earth. Like so many months before the world vanished for a short eternity. Applause and the howls of a golden retriever brought them back to the real world.

"I love you," Tony declared.

Jennifer touched his face and said, "Together, forever, and Evermore." They both ignored the flashing cameras and surrounding congratulations and walked over to the huge window where they would greet their guests and the guests would have a chance to kiss the bride.

Tony glanced outside though the plate glass and smiled. Nudging Jennifer, he motioned with his eyes to look outside.

What she saw made her mirror Tony's grin. "Angels in the sky," she whispered with a smile, hugging Tony tight. Pigeons filled the view, turning and banking in the breeze, looking like some living rice storm thrown after the wedding. The couple moved closer to the window, awed by the sight.

The rest of the group seemed to not view the pigeons as a beautiful addition to the day. Some people were muttering angrily, "Those murderers...someone get rid of them...I thought they were killed off..."

"Looks like our angels are giving us a wedding gift." Tony could not take his eyes off the birds.

Jennifer turned to him. "Our angels? You don't think any of these flew here to New York from Boston, do you?"

"Maybe, but it doesn't matter where they came from; its just perfect that they are here now." He draped his arm around Jennifer. "It makes me feel that a part of Maddie and Ben are here, wishing us well. Look... see that white one?"

Several birds had landed on the distant part of the ledge and seemed to be staring in at the festivities; one looked amazingly like Ben's Maddie. A moment later, a brown one joined it, almost landing on top of her. The white one fluttered angrily a bit, as if scolding, then they both settled down, cooing. The sight excited Jeni and Tony.

"Do you suppose...?"

"It couldn't be," Jeni exclaimed.

The bride and groom ignored their well wishers for a moment, choosing instead to reposition themselves until they were directly in front of the pair. The birds did not fly off, although the rest of their ledgemates did. The two couples eyed each other, one pair hopefully, the other with calmness and an aura of compete peace, for several long moments.

As if some unspoken conversation had ended, the birds leapt off the ledge, spreading their wings wide and joining the others in the air.

As quickly as they had appeared, the birds were gone. Only a few stranglers remained, fluttering as if slightly bewildered as to where the flock had disappeared to.

Jennifer lightly touched her crystal heart around her neck and whispered, "Thank you," to the sky. Tony nodded in agreement. Looking into each others eyes they needed no discussion. Their well-wishers awaited as did the rest of their lives.

It would be tough and times would be hard, but what was important would be there... Evermore.

ABOUT THE AUTHORS:

Hunter Lord claims to be a figment of his own imagination and few who know him would disagree. As such, he can dedicate his existence to the art of the tale, that or he likes making stories up too much to stop.

He believes that life is a sexually transmitted disease.

Ariel Masters is to be found south of the Mason-Dixon line, usually reading in some dimly-lit corner, ruining her eyesight. She is transferring her life-long passion for "a good read" to this line of novels.

A single mom and tail-end Boomer, she tries for at least one crisis a day, just to keep the adrenaline level constant.

IN A DARK ALLEY

"You stupid bitch!" Bobby shouted, the darkness in the alley providing him a haven for his display of twisted affection. "You gave it away!? Who the hell do you think you are?" He slapped the Red across her face. "I'm running a business here. I have had enough of you lately. Between this, and that sick act of yours...."

"It is not an act, Bobby," she pleaded.

"It is too. It's scaring people. They think you have AIDS."

"How do we know I don't? You won't take me to a doctor."

Bobby sneered, "Your Tuesday nooner is a doctor. He did not see anything wrong."

The statement was out of her mouth before she could stop it, safety be damned. "He is a podiatrist."

His hand lashed out again, closed fist slamming into the side of her head. Even angry, he did not want to leave visible scars... lowered the asking price.

"Don't backtalk me!" he roared.

"But I think..."

"Stupid Womber! What you think does not matter," Bobby said, pulling back for his next blow. She cringed. Before the fist could fall, a blue hand reached out, halting the strike.

"Ah, but it does," Lincoln disagreed in a deep, slow voice.

"Let go of me, lowlife! You are forgetting your place," Bobby struggled fruitlessly against his captor's grasp.

"Nope, just claiming it," Lincoln announced as he smiled and squeezed.

A loud crunch was heard, followed by screams of pain... Bobby's screams.

"You motherhumper! You broke my hand." He cradled his now useless hand, rocking himself back and forth in the alley floor's filth.

"Pity. Be thankful you have a useful one left; that's all you're going to have for entertainment from now on."

"What the frag are you talking about?" Bobby demanded through his tears and snot. Lincoln ignored him and turned to the lady of red.

"You don't want to be with him anymore, do you?" he gently questioned.

"No. But what else is there?" she whispered, half proud, half cowering in the alley ground.

"Come with me. I'll show you," He frowned. "I won't lie to you. It is going to be a hell of a hard life."

She thought, but not for long. The decision, her second solo one of the night, was easy. "It couldn't be any worse."

"Let's go, then," Lincoln said, offering her his hand. She took it.

Bobby began to object.

"You can't leave me, bitch. I own you, body and soul." He tried to sound menacing. "I will hunt you down," he growled as he staggered to his feet.

"I don't think so," Lincoln said simply. With a snap kick, he shattered Bobby's left knee; Bobby collapsed in pain.

"Will he be okay?" she asked.

"Don't worry. He will walk again, just not soon," Lincoln replied with a grim, satisfied smile.

"I was not worried, really."

From his place, again writhing among the dirt and grime, Bobby whimpered, "Please don't leave me."

The red lady turned and walked back to him. Bobby reached out for her with his good hand.

"I knew you couldn't go," Bobby said, a gleam of triumph in his eyes.

With one smooth movement, the woman of red slapped his hand to the ground and lifted her spiked heel up, smashing it down on the palm of her former master, crushing the bones. A second howl of pain tore from Bobby's throat.

Turning to Lincoln, she said, "He should not even have one good hand left for himself." Something in her manner had suddenly changed. She still walked as a timid girl, but there was a streak of pride showing through. Lincoln followed her, smiling.

Behind them, they heard Bobby murmuring "You bitch, youbitchy-ubitch..." Neither cared.

As soon as they left the alley, the skinny teenager that had been the caus
and solution to the red lady's problems ran up to the pair of Wombers.

"Is it over? Are you okay?" he asked breathlessly.

"Yes, Luke," she said. "It's over and just beginning. Are you the reaso
this man..."

"Lincoln," interrupted the blue man.

"...Lincoln came to my rescue?"

"Yes. That scum was too big for me, but I didn't want him to hurt you."

"You did good, Luke."

"You mean before?" asked Luke shyly.

"No." She smiled. "I meant now."

"Oh," said Luke, a bit of the wind taken out of his sails.

"Before, you were fantastic."

"Really?" he asked, shocked and jubilant.

"Absolutely. You were the best. And I should know."

"Wow," Luke said in wonderment. "It was my first time."

"Natural talent, I guess," she said as she kissed him on the cheek. "Take
care, you animal."

"You too," said Luke, wandering off in a daze, rubbing his cheek.

"The kid really that good?" asked Lincoln, gazing with amusement at the
departing Romeo.

"Well, let's just say, if he thinks he is, what difference does it make?"

"Nice of you."

"My nature, I guess," She quickly changed the subject, as they began to
weave through the parked cars and sleeping homeless. "What do we do
now?"

"Go underground. But first, let me ask you a question...what did he call
you?"

"What else? Bitch."

"It is important to take a new name, in order to throw off the shackles of
your old life and begin your new one with a clean slate. What would you
like your name to be?"

She thought a moment. "Some of my johns used to call me Cherry
Red."

"Kind of degrading, isn't it? The underlying references and all."

She shrugged. "I lost that a long time ago. No, it was sweet. It was
almost a term of endearment. The johns showed me more kindness and
compassion than Bobby ever did."

Lincoln argued. "But your name should help you move beyond the past."

She stood on her newfound confidence. "A name won't change how I am or what has happened in my life. I like the name."

"Then Cherry it is."

Sirens wailed like banshees in the distance. Cherry and Lincoln looked at each other and, without a word, quickened their pace. Lincoln jarred open an manhole cover, and, following freedom, they disappeared into its depths.

OUT IN THE COLD

"Please! I'm begging you. I will do anything."

"I'm sorry. I really am, but there is nothing I can do."

"There has got to be something."

"There isn't. My hands are tied."

"Untie them! I'm stage two, dammit! If I can't get in a bubble I will die. The TADS will kill me!"

"Sir, please calm down. I know what you are going through."

"Don't sit there behind your little desk with your smug little attitude and try to tell me you know what I am going through because you have no idea. Are you about to die? I don't think so. And if you were I think I would show you more compassion if I had a way of saving you."

"David..."

"Don't you dare help kill me and address me by my first name. We are not friends. To you I am Mr. Johnson."

"Mr. Johnson, GeneTechNotics is a business. We have to make money. Your insurance will not cover inclusion and we have already taken all the charity cases we can."

"I'm desperate. What can I do?"

"You can fill out a form 1110-D."

"Fine. Give me one. And let me talk to your boss.

"Trust me, it won't do any good."

"I have to try."

"The only way you are going to get into Chesire House is if Mr. Van Doff himself gets you in."

"Fine. Let me talk to him."

"No chance of that. U.S. Senators have to wait two weeks. You have not got a prayer."

"Prayer is all I've got."

"If it makes you feel any better you are not the only one we have had to turn away."

"How is that supposed to make me feel better? What should I do? Go find these people and start a support group?"

"That's not a bad idea."

"Why? So we can watch each other drop dead as our immune systems fail? So we can find someone else to care about and then leave. Go to Hell. I will save you a seat."

**COMING IN OCTOBER 1997
FROM PADWOLF PUBLISHING**

The New Novel From
HUNTER LORD and ARIEL MASTERS

WOMBERS and INNUENDOES

womb-ers *(noun, plural)*,
    1 : *life forms produced by genetic cloning using human tissue samples: considered sub-human, on a par with animals; may be bought or sold and have no rights as per various state laws which presently have been upheld by the U.S. Supreme Court; although some states accord them full human rights (see Utah);*
    recently produced Wombers are typically divided by color (done by full body tattooing) according to specialty: red (sex), blue (military/police), green (menial labor) and orange (research);

in-nu-en/does *(noun, plural)*
    1 : *insinuations, hints;*
    2 : *victims of the immune system destroying TADS virus, forced to live in sterile environments (called "Bubbles"): victims have three stages followed unequivocally by death, often from something as simple as the common cold or the flu.*

    Two groups of victims: one by birth, the other by circumstances. Both separated and barred from a full life. Innuendoes longed for a return to what they had: Wombers dreamed of a life they would never lead. Society was content to section them off from the whole, and make a buck in doing so... capitalism being still alive and well.
    But the victims had other plans...

Patrick Thomas

EXILE AND ENTRANCE

EXILE: Betrayals consumed Rick Wagner; first by his family, then by his government; each sacrificing him up for their own ends. He and nine hundred others like thousands before them.

ENTRANCE: Onto a distant planet ironically called Liberty, Rick is sold for entertainment fodder...warrior for the Tore Games, a Xile. On a sandy arena, Rick fought with friend and foe alike to the roar of alien throats...or their equivalent. It was a bizarre, frightening existence. But he was not alone.

Rick's courage and valor gain him allies in this new life. Among them a squad of fellow Xiles, a six-limbed silver wolf, a moving mountain... and Susie. An eight-year-old human child that became Rick's very reason for living. A human child whose appearance on the planet threatened the livelihood of the Muridae, ratlike slave traders that held all in their mercenary grip. She had to disappear....

The final betrayal came, not from the limbs of others, but from one of his own.

Death would have been preferred to what was planned for Susie; time was running out, and Rick was running out of hope...